TEC

ALLEN COUNTY PUBLIC LIBRARY

3 1833 04

W9-CSX-314

I hadn't really thought of my breasts as "problem breasts." It made them sound like children who wouldn't behave. Few fulfilling careers required cantaloupe boobs. And even if they did, you could always wear a Wonderbra. Victoria's Secret had yet to make an undergarment that could hide eight pounds of flesh. I looked down. No bra was going to keep these babies a secret. And those tips for the full-figured girl in the magazines? Please. Even NASA couldn't design a tank suit to camouflage my proportions.

DORIAN CIRRONE

Dancing in Red Shoes Will Kill You

HarperTrophy®
An Imprint of HarperCollinsPublishers

Harper Trophy® is a registered trademark of
HarperCollins Publishers.

Dancing in Red Shoes Will Kill You

Copyright © 2005 by Dorian Cirrone
All rights reserved. Printed in the United States of America. No part
of this book may be used or reproduced in any manner whatsoever
without written permission except in the case of brief quotations
embodied in critical articles and reviews. For information address
HarperCollins Children's Books, a division of HarperCollins
Publishers, 1350 Avenue of the Americas, New York, NY 10019.
www.harperteen.com

Library of Congress Cataloging-in-Publication Data
Cirrone, Dorian.
Dancing in red shoes will kill you / by Dorian Cirrone.—1st ed.
p.   cm.
Summary: Sixteen-year-old Kayla, a ballet dancer with very
large breasts, and her sister Paterson, an artist, are both helped and
hindered by classmates as they confront sexism, conformity, and
censorship at their high school for the arts while still managing to
maintain their sense of humor.
ISBN-10: 0-06-055703-6 — ISBN-13: 978-0-06-055703-4
[1. Sexism—Fiction.   2. Censorship—Fiction.   3.
Conformity—Fiction.   4. Ballet—Fiction.   5. Art—Fiction.   6.
Breast—Fiction.   7. High schools—Fiction.   8. Schools—
Fiction.]   I. Title.
PZ7.C499Dan   2004   2004006235
[Fic]—dc22
Typography by Sasha Illingworth

First Harper Trophy edition, 2006

In memory of my parents,
Eleanor and John Cirrone

Acknowledgments

So many people encouraged, supported, critiqued, and cajoled me during my road to publishing. If I thanked them all, this section would end up being longer than the novel. I do, however, want to acknowledge the following people:

YAWriters, Pubsters, and the entire cybercommunity of authors who freely share their knowledge and insight into the business of writing and publishing.

All the members of my writing group, in particular Heidi Boehringer, Laurie Friedman, Marjetta Geerling, Nancy Knutson, Joan Mazza, Lucille Gang Shulklapper, and Sherri Winston, for their continuous support. Kathy MacDonald and Gloria Rothstein, for their constant enthusiasm for my work. Alex Flinn, for being one of the most generous writers I know. And, of course, Joyce Sweeney, for being the greatest mentor and friend a writer could ever ask for.

My agent, Steven Chudney, for loving this novel before it was even finished. If not for his support and encouragement, I might still be on Chapter 5.

My editor, Tara Weikum, for her insight into my work, her thoughtful editing of it, and for putting it all together with such a fabulous cover. Lauren Velevis and everyone else at HarperCollins, for being so great to work with and for making my first novel so terrific.

Dr. Harris Shampain, for the best fake doctor's appointment ever and for sharing his expertise.

Bernadette Doverspike and Natalie Trees at Dance Academy of North Lauderdale, for allowing me to observe their dancers.

Mary Beth Gibson and Edvige Giunta, for guiding my earlier work and for giving me confidence when I needed it most.

Brett Kushner and Kevin Murray, for allowing me an occasional glimpse into the creativity and humor of their world. Thanks also for the driving!

Julie Arpin, for being the sister I never had and for reading every word of everything I write and telling me it's wonderful.

My daughter, Siena, for sharing her brilliance and for just being who she is.

My son, Blaise, for his humor and for giving me a glimpse into a whole new world of boy stuff.

And, lastly, my husband, Stephen Koncsol, for supporting me in all ways so that I could fulfill my dream.

I thank you all.

Dancing in Red Shoes
Will Kill You

Chapter 1

It isn't every day you walk into your sister's bedroom and find a naked guy on her bed, especially when that guy is your best friend, Joey.

Now that I've gotten your attention—it's not what you're thinking. But isn't it amazing what happens when you hear the word *naked*? The thing I didn't mention is that my sister, Paterson, is an artist, and her bedroom doubles as a studio.

My parents named her that because she was conceived in a Paterson, New Jersey, motel room about eighteen years ago. When she was younger, she used to ask why she couldn't have a normal name, like Ashley or Christine.

"You were lucky," my mother would say. "If your father had taken another road, you could have been named Secaucus Callaway."

It turned out my parents did a good thing—she's definitely not an Ashley or a Christine. She's tall and thin and her wardrobe consists mainly of various shades of black, with an occasional pair of jeans thrown in for comfort. Sometimes her hair is pink. Other times it's orange. Lately it's Electric Blue. She draws the line at piercings and tattoos because of their permanence. She says her body is an ongoing work of art.

Not too long after Paterson was born, I was conceived. It's a picture I don't want to think too much about, but it must have taken place in a pretty ordinary location because my parents named me Kayla—after nothing in particular. Just a name they both liked, with a little bit of alliteration with Callaway to satisfy my mother's enthusiasm for poetic devices.

I'd almost forgotten that Joey was coming over to model for Paterson's senior art portfolio. I knew Paterson had chosen him because he has a body most guys would kill for, but I didn't expect him to be totally naked. Or is it nude? I mean, we're talking full-frontal you-know-what with Saint Rocco hanging out and everything. Saint Rocco, by the way, is what Joey calls his penis. It must be a guy thing. I once saw an actor on *The Tonight*

Show refer to his penis as Little Elvis.

Giving proper names to private parts is something I'm pretty sure most girls do not do. I have never once heard a woman of any age refer to her vagina as Mother Teresa or Little Madonna. It just isn't done.

Anyway, once I got a quick glimpse of Saint Rocco, I put my hands over my eyes and tried to navigate past the piles of canvases and sketch pads, as well as the pastels, pencils, paints, and paintbrushes strewn all over the terra-cotta tile floor. I finally made it to a rocking chair next to the bed, behind Joey. For some reason I didn't mind looking at his butt. I get a good view of that through his tights when he's dancing in front of me in ballet class.

Joey and I have danced together since I was four and he was five. My mom put me in ballet classes because I was born with a hip defect. I don't remember, but she says I wore a cast as an infant. The doctor suggested that early ballet training might be good for me, but I don't think my parents planned on having a ballerina in the family. It was just supposed to be therapy. Joey, on the other hand, originally started with karate classes. One of the other boys' mothers owned a dance studio, and when she saw Joey do a perfect straddle split with no wincing, she offered him free lessons. Good male dancers are always in demand, even when they're only five.

Now Joey and Paterson are seniors and I'm a junior at a magnet school for the arts called Florida Arts High School, affectionately known as Farts High. You'd think at least one of the school board members might have seen that one coming.

At Farts we get to study our own individual disciplines for a couple of hours each day in addition to the usual subjects. At first my parents were afraid a high school for the arts might be a little too crunchy granola. My mom's a third-grade teacher and my dad's a psychologist, so they're both pretty traditional when it comes to education. I think they were afraid we'd forget how to add and subtract and not learn enough about the real world—whatever that is. But Paterson begged them for a whole year to let her go. They finally gave in. The next year I auditioned and was accepted into the dance program.

Paterson's a born artist. She's been drawing almost since she popped out of the womb. I don't even want to tell you about her first art project, but I'll give you a hint. It involved the inside of her diaper and the wall of her bedroom. She's always been full of surprises.

That's why I shouldn't have been too shocked to find a bare-naked Joey in Paterson's room that Saturday morning. I uncovered my eyes and made myself comfortable in the wooden rocker. Paterson, who had been watching me, poised her charcoal pencil in the air and chided, "Kayla, you are *soooo* Victorian. It's just a body."

"Yes, I know," I said. "Just flesh, blood, arteries, kidneys, intestines . . ." We'd been through this before when Paterson wanted me to pose for her figure-drawing class.

"You can wear a leotard and tights," she had said. "It'll be a good opportunity for the class to draw a body like yours."

What she meant was, with breasts like yours. From the neck down and the waist up I look a lot like Dolly Parton, though I read in a tabloid that hers were artificial, something I could never understand. Why would anyone pay for these things? It's like walking around with two quarts of milk hanging from a necklace. I have to wear three bras to dance class just to keep from hitting myself in the chin during *changements*.

There was no way I was going to pose for Paterson's classmates and let everyone stare at my body. Artists or not. Besides, I had to go to that school too, and I didn't like the idea of looking at myself in various poses hanging up in the school cafeteria, where the art students display their work. There was no way some guy was going to salivate over my breasts while scarfing down a salami-and-cheese sub.

I was imagining one of the more Neanderthal guys in

school with vinegar-and-oil dressing dribbling down his chin when Joey broke in: "How's the view from back there?"

"Not bad," I said, noticing Joey was one pale color from the top of his neck to his heels. No tan line at all. Only his dark brown hair broke the monotone.

"You've got to get out in the sun," I said. "You look like the Pillsbury Doughboy with muscles. You could never be in one of those Coppertone ads where the dog pulls down your towel—there'd be no difference."

"Too bad," Joey said. "If I don't get into a ballet company next year, I'm hoping to be the first gay Coppertone guy. I can see it on billboards now," he said, holding up an imaginary bottle of suntan lotion and coyly pulling up an invisible beach towel behind him. "When you come out of the closet, make sure you bring your Coppertone."

I laughed and leaned back in the rocking chair. Joey had come out a few years before, and it hadn't been that big a deal for him. I'm not saying all male ballet dancers are gay, because they're not. Or that Joey's family was happy about it at first. But his parents and friends had had a pretty good idea about it all along. At a place like Farts, being gay is not all that unusual.

I was starting to get bored after a while, but I didn't have anything better to do. We were having auditions for

Cinderella in a few days, and I couldn't concentrate on anything else.

I put my feet up on Paterson's paint-splattered denim bedspread, inched forward, and poked Joey in the back with my big toe.

"Yow! Your toe feels like sandpaper," he yelled.

"Yours would too if you had to dance in pointe shoes for hours."

Joey squirmed. "I am *so* glad that's never caught on for men."

"What about the stepmother in *Cinderella*?" I reminded him. "That's almost always played by a man on pointe. You may end up with that part next week."

"I'm more the Prince Charming type," Joey said.

Paterson, who usually doesn't talk much while she's sketching, broke in. "You know, in an early version of the fairy tale, women actually cut off their toes to try to squeeze their feet into the glass slipper—just so they could marry the stupid prince."

"Gross," I said. "It's a good thing it wasn't a satin pump. Can you imagine how it would have looked by the time he got to Cinderella?"

Paterson smiled as she swept her pencil across the paper.

I picked up one of her art books and flipped through it. The book was filled with pictures of nude women, but hardly any men. In fact, the only men I could find seemed to be Satan and Adam. In one of the pictures, Satan was looking pretty good. I flipped to another before things got too weird.

"Look at how fat these women were," I said.

"No one thought they were fat," Paterson said. "They were considered beautiful with all that flesh. No offense, but they probably would have thought all those muscles of yours were ugly."

I looked down at my right leg, pointed my toe, and watched my calf bulge into a little ball. I was proud of my muscles. I had worked hard for them. How many times a day had I done *pliés, relevés, tendus*? Hundreds. Sometimes I wondered if it was all worth it. I never seemed to get a lead role. For two years I'd landed parts in the corps, the group of dancers in long skirts dancing in between the principals' spectacular solos and their *pas de deux*.

I hoped things would be different this year. I was a junior now, and I had spent the entire summer perfecting my technique. While a lot of the dancers at Farts had taken class only a few hours a week, I'd spent eight weeks in New York, studying six hours a day at the American School of Ballet.

I was imagining myself in a tutu, dancing a solo, when Paterson announced, "You know, I've never sketched an uncircumcised male nude."

I dropped the art book on my big toe.

"Uh, thanks for noticing?" Joey said. "My parents were ex-hippies when I was born, and my father thought it was a barbaric custom."

"He did have a point," Paterson said, adding, "Oops, sorry for the pun."

I picked up the book, rubbed my toe, and began leafing through the pages again. I didn't want any part of this conversation, puns or no puns. It was just way too much information.

Things were quiet for a few minutes, and I could tell Paterson was thinking. "You know," she said, "I could circumcise you."

I dropped the book again.

"Excuse me?" Joey said. "But it sounded like you said you could circumcise me, and that couldn't possibly be what I heard."

Paterson looked up from the sketch pad. "Not literally, of course."

"Of course," Joey said.

Paterson put down her pencil and clapped her hands. "Let's have a bris."

Joey sat upright and crossed his legs. "A what?"

"It's when a Jewish baby boy is eight days old, and they do the circumcision in front of everyone at a big party," I explained.

"Whoa." Joey's voice raised an octave. "You're kidding. A party?"

Paterson opened the top drawer of her dresser and pulled out a small white object and a huge purple scarf. She threw the scarf around her shoulders and unfolded the white silky thing, which I recognized as a yarmulke she had taken from our cousin's bar mitzvah. At the time I had reminded her they were just for the men. "Why should they get everything?" she'd said, reaching into the basket at the temple.

She put the yarmulke on her head. "It's a few years late," she told Joey, "but, hey, it's never too late for a party."

Joey covered his crotch with a pillow. "This is one party I could do without. And, by the way, don't you have to have some training in this? And aren't you supposed to be Jewish at least?"

Paterson leaned toward her art box to get something. "My father's mother is Jewish. That makes me one . . ." She thought for a second and shook her head. "One-somethingth Jewish."

"One fourth," I said. I've always been a little better in math.

Paterson lifted a huge eraser in the air and announced. "Behold, the holy instrument." She turned the easel toward us and began erasing Joey's penis.

3 1833 04769 709 6

Joey curled into a fetal position. "The pain, the pain," he cried in a voice that was supposed to sound like a baby's, but sounded more like a really bad opera diva. I was laughing so hard that tears came to my eyes. I doubled over in the rocking chair and screamed, "Stop, you're killing me." Then I grabbed a pillow from the back of the bed and beat Joey over the head with it.

Meanwhile Paterson remained unfazed by the performance, lost in her world of simulated surgery. When she finished, there was a blank spot on the sketch pad where Joey's penis had been.

Joey stopped screaming to see what she'd done. "Please," he shouted, "fill it in, quick. It hurts to even look at it."

Paterson picked up the charcoal pencil and quickly sketched a circumcised penis in place of where Joey's had been. "There," she said, pointing to the sketch. "And now I present you with a boy who is a cut above the rest."

I groaned as Joey yelled, "Ouch! That hurts even more than the fake circumcision."

"Thank you. Thank you," Paterson said with a bow, ignoring our lack of enthusiasm for her jokes. "Applause will do fine. No tips, please."

Joey was rolling on the bed, moaning and laughing at the same time, when I spotted an old sketch Paterson had done of me. "Hey," I said. "Can you do that for me—you know, plastic surgery by charcoal pencil?"

Paterson picked up the sketch. "Sure, why not. What do you want me to do?"

"Make my boobs smaller."

Paterson laid Joey's picture on the floor and sat mine up on the wooden easel.

"I'm warning you," Joey said. "It'll hurt."

I laughed and watched as Paterson waved the eraser over my chest. She made a few scribbles on the paper and . . .

"Voila," she said. "Size thirty-four B."

"Wow," I whispered. I couldn't believe it. My light brown hair was still pulled back into a bun and my face was the same, but I looked so different—way thinner and more all-American girl. Much more like a ballerina.

I was staring at the stranger that was me when Joey broke in. "*Hello*, remember the naked boy on the bed. Could we finish up with The Picture of Dorian Gray and get back to me?"

"The picture of who?" I said.

Joey started to explain, but I was only half listening. I couldn't stop staring at the sketch.

Chapter 2

I struggled as I slipped my arms through the straps of
my third heavy-duty, all-purpose sports bra and
pulled it down over the other two. Then I hiked up
my camisole leotard with the reinforced straps over that.
I took a deep breath to make sure I still could, given the
contraptions I was forced to wear in order to keep my
upper body from looking like two giant Jell-O molds.

I liked getting to the dressing room before everyone
else so I could put my leotard and tights on in private,
without everyone gawking at me. Apparently my breasts
are so freakish that even straight girls feel comfortable
enough to stare.

Despite the extra time it took to get ready, the smell

of the dressing room was always comforting—the mingled odors of feet, sweat, leather dance bags, and the occasional scent of elastic from a new pair of tights, fresh out of the plastic bag.

I did a few ballet steps in the mirror and checked the relative motion of my breasts. Just as I finished my third *jeté*, I heard the voice.

"Hang on everyone. This one's a seven point five on the Richter scale."

Melissa Edwards. Her voice, and everything else about her, had been haunting me since kindergarten.

My first instinct was to hurl a can of hairspray at her, but I reminded myself that in a little over a year I'd be free of her forever. I faced her and squeezed out a fake smile.

She dropped her dance bag on the wooden bench. "Big audition week, huh, KC?"

Melissa had this annoying habit of calling everyone by their initials. I was pretty sure she did it so she could use her own initials all the time. It was like she had a license to write ME, ME, ME, all over everything— notebooks, pointe shoes, dance bags, everything.

My relationship with Melissa was based on our mutual love for ballet, as well as our mutual mistrust of each other. It all started when we were in our first ballet class together at Miss Penny's School of Dance. We were

in the same recital number, a rendition of that great clas-
sical ballet *Little Miss Muffet*. Our costumes consisted of
red tutus and red spray-painted ballet shoes. We were
each given a tuffet, or more accurately a little white
wooden stool, designed to distract the audience from
noticing we didn't know much actual ballet. We were
supposed to dance around the tuffets and every once in
a while return to them in a cute pose. The dance was to
end with one final extravaganza in which we spun with
our arms over our heads and ran back to our tuffets as a
large cardboard spider dropped from the rafters.

No one was ever really sure what happened, but
somehow Melissa and I ran for the same tuffet, turning
the final tableau into one big game of musical chairs.
Being a bit larger in the buttocks area than Melissa, I
succeeded in knocking her off the stool and onto the
stage floor, at which time she began screaming words
that an auditorium of parents were unaccustomed to
hearing from a five-year-old. I, on the other hand, held
my pose with a big smile as the curtain raced shut in
front of us.

The official videotape captured it all, except for who
was at fault. The camera guy apparently thought we were
so cute, he zoomed in to get a close-up of our dueling
derrières. We never found out if the empty tuffet was to
the right or the left.

After the show Melissa's mother promised my parents she'd "get to the bottom of it." Later my mother, who wasn't much of a stage mother even then, laughed about the whole thing. She said she pictured Melissa and her parents watching the video over and over in slow motion, freeze-framing it in certain places like CIA agents trying to catch the real assassin.

That was the first sign of Melissa's competitive nature. What began as a mere kindergarten scuffle evolved into a full-fledged rivalry once Melissa realized I could match her leap for leap and extension for extension. From then on, fueled by a pushy mother and a mean streak the length of a hundred pointe shoes lying toe to heel, Melissa has tried to sabotage every good thing that's come my way.

Case in point: second grade. A Valentine sent to me by Richie Cruz is mysteriously intercepted. Later it's passed around the room for everyone to laugh at, sending a red-faced Richie to the rest room and thus ending the short, happy life of my first romance.

Third grade. Miss Penny's recital, Hawaiian Holiday. The pin holding my grass skirt to the back of my leotard becomes unfastened just as I'm about to go onstage. After swaying my hips a few times, the grass skirt ends up bunched between my legs. Guess whose hula hands were behind me when I was waiting in the wings?

For several years every recital held a new surprise. Torn tights. Missing headpieces. As I got older, I learned how to lock up my stuff and keep it away from Melissa. But even now I'm cautious of her—always waiting for the other pointe shoe to drop.

I zipped my dance bag and threw it in my locker. Before Melissa had a chance to crack any more stupid boob jokes, the rest of the girls in Miss Alicia's sixth-period ballet class began pouring in. Half were chattering about the upcoming auditions for *Cinderella*, while the other half seemed equally excited about someone named Gray.

"Oh my God, did you see how cute he was?" Ivy Thompson said, dropping her dance bag in a locker next to mine.

"Who?" I said.

"The new guy who transferred here from somewhere up north this semester. He's got the cutest eyebrows."

Ivy has a thing for eyebrows and it is the first feature she notices on everyone, including me, which is pretty amazing. Mine, by the way, are okay with her, but could be a little thinner.

"Where did you see him?" I said.

Melissa looked away from the mirror where she had been studying her sideways silhouette, so thin and flat it was almost nonexistent. "He just started working in the school store. I needed new pointe shoes, and he waited on me."

Yeah, sure, I thought. Melissa had a bag full of pointe shoes that were in great condition.

"I got the whole story," she said. "His mom's poet-in-residence at the university this semester. She'll be doing some public readings and, being the lover of poetry that I am, I told him I'd go."

"Oh," I said, "and who is your favorite poet again—Mater Goose?"

Melissa went back to basking in her own reflection. "I never even heard of him," she said.

I could always count on Melissa being so self-absorbed that she didn't even get it when the joke was on her.

She pulled out her American lit book and pointed to the cover. "This is my favorite poet. It's Gray's, too."

"Walt Whitman?"

"Gray's favorite poem is 'Song of Myself,' Melissa said, adding, "It's my favorite too."

I adjusted my leotard strap one more time. "Why doesn't that surprise me?"

"You know," Melissa said, "if I weren't a dancer, I think I'd probably be a poet."

I snapped my locker shut and spun the dial. "Excuse me while I go barf."

Ivy, who was adjusting the elastic on her ballet shoes,

leaned over and looked at the cover of Melissa's English book. "Hmm, Walt Whitman—he's got some nice eyebrows."

It was a relief to finally get to the barre and start class. Miss Alicia dragged a chair to the middle of the room and rested her hand on the back of it. While she demonstrated a *plié* combination, I crossed my eyes at Joey in the mirror. It was a secret sign we devised when we were in elementary school. The eyes are the only part of the body you can signal with and not get into trouble in ballet class.

Miss Alicia was nearly fifty years old and married with two children, but we still called her *Miss*, along with her first name. It's one of those ballet studio traditions, like dancing on your toes or turning your feet out like a duck. No one messes with it. It had been a long time since she'd danced professionally. Now she was about ten pounds overweight, twenty-five if you're talking ballet pounds.

Miss Alicia started the music and sat with her legs in second position. While she rested her hands on each knee and held her elbows to the sides, her head moved up and down as we lowered ourselves into *grande pliés* and then straightened up again.

I looked at myself in the mirror as we held the final

relevé. My eyes traveled from the floor up, doing the ritual inventory: heels high, knees straight, hips turned out, back straight, stomach in, shoulders down. Everything was perfect except you know what, where I looked like a hard-boiled egg that had been cooked too long and the white stuff was bulging out in great big poofs, beyond the boundaries of the shell.

Ivy was in front of me and Melissa was in front of her. They both had perfect ballet bodies. Melissa didn't even have to wear a bra with her leotard, and Ivy was fine with a flimsy thing from Victoria's Secret. It felt like I'd skipped that phase entirely, going from the stretchy training bra with the pink bow in the middle straight to the steel underwire and two-inch straps. I'd even grown another full cup size the summer before junior year, bringing my bra size up to a double D.

"Tight fifth position, tight, tight, tight," Miss Alicia said. "Hold . . . hold . . . and down."

She changed the music and demonstrated the next combination with her arms and hands. I watched the big blue ring on her right index finger as she pretended her hand was a foot, pointing and lifting to the staccato piano notes. She often pantomimed the steps she wanted us to do, but every once in a while she would use her legs and feet in such a spectacular way that we were all reminded of her former greatness. I couldn't imagine how it felt not to dance onstage anymore.

Once we finished at the barre, Miss Alicia broke from the usual class schedule and asked us to sit in the center of the room.

"I have some announcements." She turned the chair around and sat with her arms resting on the back. "As you all know, at the end of the week we will have auditions for *Cinderella*."

Murmurs swept across the studio.

"The good news is that there will be parts for everyone. Of course, some parts are not as large as others, but every part is important to the overall ballet."

Knowing chuckles mixed in with the murmurs. Someone sitting a few rows behind me whispered in a Spanish accent, mimicking Miss Alicia, "There are no small parts, just small ballet dancers." Another voice answered, "Yeah, small ballet dancers with fat asses." Another voice, which I immediately recognized, chimed in, "Or gigantic boobs."

I pretended not to hear Melissa's comment, even though I could see her face in the mirror.

Miss Alicia frowned at the class for a few seconds and then continued. "In some versions of *Cinderella*, the stepmother and stepsisters are played by men for comic effect. Because we have a lack of male dancers, the only female part played by a man will be the part of the stepmother."

"That part's for Joey," yelled Devin Demanne, the only other male dancer in the advanced class.

"I wouldn't think of robbing you of your greatest role," Joey deadpanned back.

Miss Alicia clapped three times. "Enough, enough," she said. "There will be none of that. The choosing of parts will be very objective. A choreographer from Ballet on the Beach has agreed to stage the ballet and will be completely in charge of auditions. If you want a principal role, I suggest you begin working on the extension of your legs rather than your mouths."

Immediately everyone began stretching in some way or another. Legs sprang open and arms reached forward until chests were lying flat on the ground. Other legs stretched to the ceiling as knees tried to meet foreheads. Great extensions were one way to stand out at the audition. And to get great extensions, you needed the stretch as well as the strength.

"I see you've gotten my message," Miss Alicia said. "From now until the auditions, don't waste any of your time." She clapped three times again. "Now stand for the center work."

Once she had taught us the combination of steps, we danced in small groups. When it was my turn to rest against the barre and watch, I surveyed the competition. There were several worthy contenders: Melissa, Ivy,

Lourdes—a senior who, like Joey, planned to postpone college and go straight to a ballet company after graduation—and a couple of others who weren't consistently excellent but could appeal to someone who hadn't seen them dance day after day.

Getting a lead part was definitely going to be tough.

After class I waited for Joey in front of the girl's dressing room. As he approached, Devin trailed behind him. "Don't think the gay guy always gets the girl," he said. "In this ballet it'll be different."

"I don't always get the girl," Joey said, putting his arm around me. "Just the one you want."

"Shut up, you fa—," Devin shouted, stopping himself as the band director walked by.

Ever since freshman year, Devin had resented Joey and me—me, for not going out with him, and Joey, for being his biggest ballet competitor. He tried to use the gay thing against Joey, but it always backfired—no one listened to his stupid jokes.

Joey laughed as Devin stormed off. "Let's go find Paterson," he said.

Aside from the dance studio, the art room was my favorite place in the school. Artwork hung on every available wall space, and wherever you turned you could find something beautiful to stare at. Paterson was working on a sketch of Lourdes, who had modeled for the figure-drawing class. "I can't get this ribbon right," she muttered before she even knew we were there.

"What are you talking about?" Joey said. "It's great."

"No, it's not right," Paterson said. She took the eraser and removed the whole pointe shoe. Lourdes sat with a stump at the end of her leg.

I surveyed the other work surrounding Paterson's easel. "Hey, where's the picture of Joey?"

"I'm saving that one," Paterson said.

"For what?" Joey asked, affecting a scholarly inflection. "New York's famed Metropolitan Museum of Art?"

"I wish," Paterson said. "I'm waiting till everything's finished to turn in the whole portfolio." She picked up her sketch pencil. "Can you guys occupy yourselves for a while before I drive us home . . . please?"

Joey and I looked at each other. We were always waiting for Paterson to finish something, but it was better than taking the bus.

"C'mon," Joey said, "let's go to the school store and check out the new guy."

"Not you too?" I said. "Melissa and Ivy are already in love. What did you hear?"

"Just that his sexual persuasion wasn't immediately identifiable."

"And you learned this how?" Paterson asked.

Joey looked at the floor. "I admit it wasn't a very good source. . . . It was Devin."

Paterson groaned. "Mr. Homophobe himself. I'd be a little skeptical of anything Devin had to say."

"Don't you remember?" I said. "After I refused to go out with him, he tried to spread a rumor that I had implants."

"Well, if one of us doesn't get a date soon," Joey said, "there'll be even more rumors." He turned toward me. "Maybe you can go out with the new guy and get some fresh blood into this triumvirate."

"Okay, we'll check him out," I said. If there was someone at Farts worth dating, I definitely wanted to see it for myself. I turned to Paterson, who was trying to reconstruct Lourdes's left foot. "Fifteen minutes, okay?"

Inside the school store, I didn't see anyone who looked like the hot guy I'd been hearing about. I was surveying the lamb's wool and various types of toe pads when Joey called me over. "Look at this," he said, gesturing toward a poster on the wall next to the tights.

Attention Dancers:
The school store has many of your needs.
Leg warmers, leotards
toe shoes, tights

ice packs, Ace bandages
tape and gauze.
But, we're sorry to say,
we're all out of applause.

"Very cute," I said. "It makes us sound like a bunch of masochistic egotists."

"That wasn't how I meant it."

Joey and I spun around. I stared into the eyes of the speaker and immediately knew he had to be Gray. My next thought was that the name Gray was all wrong for him. It was too bland, too flat, too insipid. His eyes looked at the poem and then back to me. With those eyes he should have been named Aquamarine, Cerulean, Indigo. Yes, that was it, Indigo.

"I'm Gray Foster," he said. "I didn't mean to offend the dancers. It's just a poem I put together while I was looking at the inventory list."

I laughed self-consciously. "I was just kidding," I said. "I'm a *big* fan of poetry." Ugh. I was just as bad as Melissa. The only poetry I'd read was in English class.

While Joey introduced himself, I did my own inventory: dark wavy hair pulled back in a ponytail, good body (not as good as Joey's, but good), and those eyes, whoa. I really hoped Devin was wrong.

"Can I help you find something?" Gray said.

"Uh . . . umm." Suddenly I couldn't remember what I was looking for.

"Didn't you want some lamb's wool?" Joey said.

"Yeah, lamb's wool," I said, "for my pointe shoes." How stupid did that sound? Of course it was for my pointe shoes, or maybe I was going to make a sweater with it.

Gray picked up a small plastic packet with some kind of gel inside it. "We just got these in," he said. "Some of the dancers are using them instead of lamb's wool or foam rubber pads."

Joey picked one up and squished it between his fingers. "They look like breast implants."

I shot him a look, the kind I usually reserved for Melissa. Then I quickly glanced at Gray to see if his eyes were on my breasts. Surprisingly, they weren't. He was looking at my face. Was that a good sign?

"I think I'd rather stick to the lamb's wool," I said.

Gray bent over to get a fresh box out of the cabinet. Joey and I took the opportunity to check out his butt.

I was in a daze by the time I pulled out my wallet to pay for the lamb's wool, captivated by Gray's looks and charm. I could have forked over two week's allowance and not even known it. By the time Joey and I got out of the store, Joey had invited Gray to watch the auditions for *Cinderella* and I'd professed a deep love for poetry as well as the desire to attend one of his mother's readings.

"So what did you two think about the new guy?" Paterson said as she steered her Jetta out of the parking lot.

"I think Devin might have been right," I said.

"No way," Joey answered.

I turned toward the backseat. "I'm serious. He didn't even look at my boobs when you made that crack about breast implants. And, by the way, what was that all about?"

Joey shrugged. "I'm sorry. They looked like implants. It was the first thing that came to my mind."

"Where have you seen breast implants?" Paterson said.

"On one of those TV specials where they show you things like liposuction and plastic surgery. They made little slits around the woman's nipple and—"

"Okay, that's enough," I said. "We believe you. Let's get back to why you don't think he's gay."

"Oh, that," Joey said. "He was checking you out like crazy when you weren't looking. He's a typical guy, just better at it than most. Too bad. He's really good looking."

"I'm sorry," I said, secretly shouting *hurray* inside.

"That's okay," Joey said. "I've got to focus on getting into a ballet company this year anyway. He'd just be a distraction."

I put my head back on the leopard print headrest and for a few minutes forgot about the next day's auditions. I was definitely ready for a distraction like Gray Foster.

Chapter 3

We were almost at the end of English lit when my name came booming over the PA system. "Ms. Halstrom, could you please send Kayla Callaway to the guidance office?"

Immediately everyone's eyes turned my way as an undercurrent of curious looks rippled across the classroom. A couple of voices from the back sang an exaggerated "Ooooh."

I looked at Ms. Halstrom, hoping she could provide a clue as to why, for the first time in my entire sixteen years, I was being called to see a guidance counselor. If it were senior year, it would be different; she'd want to talk about college. But at Farts everyone knew the guidance counselors were so overworked that, if you were called in during any other year, you had to be either dyslexic or on drugs. To my knowledge, I wasn't either.

Ms. Halstrom looked back at me with curiosity and surprise. I could tell she was already making up some scenario in her head. English teachers like to find all kinds of hidden meaning in things.

But all she said was, "You'd better take your backpack. We're almost ready to change classes."

Halfway to the guidance counselor, I began to get excited. I knew I hadn't done anything wrong, so I started fantasizing about what she could possibly want to tell me. Maybe there was a dance scholarship she wanted to recommend. Or maybe there was some award that I'd been nominated for and didn't know about. Auditions for *Cinderella* were that afternoon. But I knew it couldn't have anything to do with getting a part because the dance department always handled that.

The guidance office was bigger than I'd expected it to be. I had to stop at a front desk and give my name before I was directed to another, smaller office. Inside a heavy-set woman stood and introduced herself as Ms. Marone. Behind her head—which reeked of way too much hair spray—a huge poster displaying a waterfall and a rainbow read: IF YOU CAN DREAM IT, YOU CAN ACHIEVE IT. I hoped her advice wasn't as clichéd as her taste in posters.

She pointed to a chair across from her desk. "Sit down," she said as if she were a doctor ready to give some depressing news about my test results.

She sat behind her dark wooden desk and folded her hands on a green blotter. "Kayla, do you know why I called you in here?"

I was pretty sure the dumb look on my face told the answer, but I managed to vocalize an "Umm, no."

"You have no idea?"

I could tell by her tone of voice and the guessing game that there was no scholarship or award. I tried to think of the answer she was looking for. "Well, my grades are good. I'm keeping up with the advanced ballet class. I haven't joined many clubs, I know, but the dance program is pretty demanding. . . ." I knew I was rambling, but she sat there, silent, looking at me like I was some sort of lab rat.

She looked down at a piece of paper and nodded. "Yes, your grades are good. And I see you're doing well in the dance program, but . . ."

I didn't like the sound of that "but." I stared at the jar of Jolly Ranchers on her desk, watching the light shine through the bright colors.

"Would you like one?" Ms. Marone said.

I looked up, startled. "Uh, no thanks."

Ms. Marone nodded and gave me a knowing look.

What was that supposed to mean? Did she think I had false teeth?

She folded her hands again. "You know, you have some very good friends." She paused.

I felt an obligation to fill in the silence. "Yes, very good," I said. But was that the reason she'd called me in? Was this the day to call in everyone with very good friends? Shouldn't there have been more people then?

Ms. Marone nodded. "These friends of yours care very much about you. . . ."

I felt a lump rising in my throat. I still wasn't sure what I'd done, but I was beginning to feel really guilty about it.

"And they're very concerned about . . ."

Suddenly I knew what she was talking about. I'd been at a party the week before with Joey and Paterson, and I'd taken a sip of someone's beer. I was just about to blurt out that it was only a sip and I didn't even like it, when she finished her sentence.

". . . your bulimia."

"My what?" I was all set to confess to ingesting a teaspoon of alcohol. But bulimia? That was like the total opposite of ingesting. Maybe she'd gotten me confused with one of the other dancers.

"It's okay," she whispered. "It's natural to deny it. Bulimia is one of those hidden diseases that no one wants to admit to. That's why it's good that your friends came forward."

"But I'm not bulimic," I said.

"It's okay. You can talk about it here," she said. "This is a safe place for you to discuss your emotions."

She seemed so caring and professional. I began to wonder if maybe I *was* bulimic and just didn't know it. I racked my mind to think of the last time I'd vomited. There was that time in eighth grade that I ate a bad corn dog in the school cafeteria and lost it all over Nicky McNerny during last period and, before that, in fourth grade, when I woke up with a stomach virus and threw up in my bed. That didn't seem like enough times to qualify as bulimia. In fact, vomiting was something I found really disgusting, not anything I'd do voluntarily or on a regular basis.

"You know," Ms. Marone continued, "I recently read some startling statistics about the ballet world—as many as fifteen percent of dancers suffer from a serious eating disorder. And, one out of two has some struggle with eating." She whispered, as if she were in church. "So you're not alone."

I could see she had done her homework. I wanted to scream out that I was the other one out of the two—not the one with the disorder, the one that ate enough and kept it all down. But it was obvious she'd already pegged me as a barfing ballerina. My eating habits were suspect until my food was proven digested.

Ms. Marone continued to regale me with tales of ballet and bulimia. "You know," she continued, "I've read that every few years, they have to change the pipes in the bathroom at one ballet company in New York because the stomach acid from the girls throwing up erodes the metal."

I bit my upper lip to keep from laughing at the vision in my head of dancers lined up in their tutus retching in choreographed unison at the open stalls. Just then the bell rang, and my thoughts immediately turned to the auditions. Like Cinderella at midnight, I realized I had a deadline. I grabbed my backpack. "I've got auditions this afternoon, and I've got to get to ballet class this period to warm up. I can't be late."

"But we're not finished discussing your . . . problem," Ms. Marone said.

"I'm sorry," I answered more emphatically, "but I have auditions."

I slipped into class in the middle of a *plié* combination and mouthed the word *sorry* to Miss Alicia. She looked at me in a sympathetic way. Had she known where I'd been? Was she in on this bogus bulimia conspiracy? I went through the whole barre warm-up, looking at everyone's reflection in the mirror in a different way than I usually did. This time I wasn't comparing my extensions or the arch in my foot. I was looking for "friends."

After ruling out most of the class, including Miss Alicia, who I knew would have approached me first, it all came down to the usual suspects—Devin and Melissa.

Devin definitely had it in for me, especially if he thought I was interested in Gray Foster. Had he seen Joey and me talking to Gray in the bookstore? Ms. Marone had said "friends" were concerned about me. Had Devin and Melissa teamed up for this *pas de deux* of deception?

I couldn't let it occupy my mind. After class we were all going over to the auditorium for the audition. I had to be ready physically and mentally. How could I dance like Cinderella when I felt like an evil stepsister inside?

From the stage, the auditorium looked pretty empty except for the people from Ballet on the Beach and some others who had come by to watch. I looked around for Gray, but it was hard to see who was sitting in the back. I wasn't sure if I really wanted him there. His presence would have definitely proven he was interested. But then again, I was nervous enough dancing for the judges. I didn't need the added pressure.

Everyone in the dance program was crowded onto

the stage, sitting and listening to a guy named Timm, "with two *em*s," explain the history of the ballet. I wasn't sure why he told us about the two *em*s. I heard him say something about Prokofiev, but after that I tuned out. I was imagining myself as Cinderella at the ball when Ivy leaned over and whispered to me, "Are you okay?"

We were sitting in the back so Timm with two *em*s couldn't see us. I turned to her and whispered, "Yeah, why?"

"You know," she said.

I was beginning to suspect I knew, but I played dumb. "No, I don't, what do you mean?"

"You know," she repeated. She took her index finger and motioned it toward her open mouth.

"It was *you*?" I blurted out.

Timm inserted a *shhh* into his speech.

I lowered my voice and talked through my teeth, trying to keep my lips still. "Why did you tell Ms. Marone I was bulimic?"

"We just wanted to help," Ivy whispered.

"*We?*"

"Yes. Melissa and me."

"And why did Melissa think I was bulimic?" I said, trying not to scream.

"Remember in the locker room the other day when you said, 'Excuse me while I go barf'?"

I dropped my head into my hands. Ivy was a bigger idiot than I thought she was, and Melissa apparently was a more devious enemy than I thought *she* was. I understood now what was going on. Melissa must have hoped I'd either be stuck in Ms. Marone's office or, at the very least, be too upset to do my best at the auditions. And she'd gotten poor, dumb, eyebrow-loving Ivy involved in the whole thing too. Well, I'd show her. I lifted my head and turned toward Ivy. "That's just an expression," I whispered, calmly.

Her eyes opened wide. "It is?" Looking confused, she slumped and added, "I'm really sorry."

I didn't answer her. I was trying to figure out how to let Melissa know her little scheme wasn't going to work. Or maybe it was better to pretend for a while that I didn't know it was she who had spilled the bogus bulimia beans, and then go in for the kill when the time was right?

I tuned back into Timm's speech. He explained that he'd be conducting the auditions for the judges sitting in the audience. We would first learn two combinations together and then do them in groups. After that we would be paired up to perform a *pas de deux*. Ivy leaned toward me one last time. "He could stand to tweeze a little, huh?" she whispered.

Timm instructed us to stand and get ready to learn

the first combination. Simultaneously all the girls, including me, pulled down our leotards, which had crawled up our butts while we were sitting. It looked as if it was part of the choreography.

Timm had brought a couple of dancers with him to teach us the steps. Both girls looked like waifs, which was in contrast to Timm, who looked like he'd been hitting the Häagen-Dazs a little too much lately.

The first combination was fairly easy—an assortment of basic steps, ending in a double *pirouette*. We learned it in one big group, walking through the steps and practically falling over one another. I was glad Melissa was on the other side of the stage. I might have been tempted to accidentally land on her foot.

Once we learned the steps, Timm had us do them in four groups of eight. Melissa and Ivy were in the first group with Joey. Lourdes was in the second group. Devin was in the third. And I was in the fourth. I was glad I'd get a chance to watch Joey as well as the major competition.

Melissa and Ivy clearly were the best dancers in their group, excluding Joey, who managed to fit a quadruple *pirouette* in at the end. I looked at Timm to see his reaction. He nodded and smiled as Joey walked to the wings.

Once the second group moved forward, Melissa inched her way toward me as I stood against the back curtain. She leaned over and whispered, loud enough so I could hear her above the music and the clunking of pointe shoes, "Lourdes is getting fat, don't you think?"

Wasn't that just like her? Pretending to be my friend now so she could knock out more of the competition. I guessed it was some kind of weird compliment that she put me in the same league as Lourdes. I ignored her, but she just kept talking.

"I heard she might be pregnant."

I turned toward Melissa and scowled. If she thought she was going to rope me into her petty rivalries the way she had roped Ivy in, she was mistaken.

I watched the second and third groups in silence. I knew why Melissa wanted to get Lourdes out of the race. She was definitely the most Cinderella-like. Her huge brown eyes had an innocence, as well as a sadness, about them. Her mother had sent her to Miami from Cuba with an aunt and some cousins when she was ten years old. They had planned to bring the rest of the family soon after, but it had been seven years since she had seen her parents or her two brothers. How could Melissa even think about trashing Lourdes? What went on in her warped little mind?

Devin's group had a few freshmen and sophomores who could have been in the running for some of the good parts. Usually, though, Miss Alicia made sure the best dancers who had paid their dues in the corps for a couple of years were rewarded. I figured it was my turn for a reward. I'd worked harder than ever since the school year started.

By the time my turn came, I was psyched. The combination was fairly easy, so I was able to show off my extensions. I tried to look Cinderella-like and show the kind of emotion the part called for. When it was over, I was afraid I might have looked more indignant than sad over not being able to go to the ball. But I knew I'd danced well.

The second combination was more difficult—several *grands jetés*, *arabesques*, and turns. This time Timm asked to see it in groups of four. "Spread out," he said. "Let's see you really move. Take over the stage."

Joey was unbelievable, as usual, taking Timm's words literally. Leaps and turns were his strengths. He gave it everything he had, soaring higher and farther than everyone else, spinning and stopping without wavering an inch. It was as if he was powered by invisible strings from heaven. I glanced at Timm, who couldn't take his eyes off Joey's dancing.

As the four dancers walked back toward the curtain, sweating and breathing heavily, I gave Joey a thumbs-up. Another four went forward, then another four. Melissa and Ivy were in separate groups. Neither of them had great leaps, but both displayed beautiful *arabesques* as they lifted their legs in back, higher than anyone else. I hated to admit it, but despite Ivy's vapidness and Melissa's villainy, they could both dance like angels.

The velvet curtain behind me fluttered each time someone moved against it. My stomach started doing the same thing. That's all I'd have to do, I thought, lose my lunch right here and confirm Ms. Marone's suspicions. I avoided any eye contact with Melissa.

The stakes were getting higher. Lourdes was in the next group and, of course, did everything perfectly. I tried to be happy for her. I thought of Melissa and how she wanted Lourdes and me out of the picture. I wasn't going to let her get her wish. As I watched Devin's group, my adrenaline started to kick in. All four were good, including the younger dancers. I was beginning to feel more of a rush.

By the time I stepped forward to take my place, I felt like I was ready to run a marathon. I had never been so ready to dance. Somehow my turns were cleaner and my leaps had more power behind them. Even my *arabesques* seemed to be higher than usual. I guessed that was what revenge felt like.

Joey mouthed, "Wow" to me as I walked back to the curtain.

For the last part of the audition, Timm taught us a

pas de deux that he danced with one of the waif girls. He was stronger and way more graceful than I thought he'd be. But as soon as he finished dancing, he took a small brush out of his pocket and combed the hair in back of his head to cover a bald spot. I figured no matter how successful you were, there was always some insecurity ready to rear its head—balding or not.

Since the only guys were Joey, Devin, and two more sophomores, each had to do the combination seven times. I held my breath for a few seconds while Timm announced the groups. Fortunately, I was paired with Joey. I knew he had the strength to help me show off my best work, and besides, he was the only one I could count on not to cop a feel.

When it was our turn, Joey really came through—lifting me with ease and steadying me during the *pirouettes* and *penchée*. By the time we finished, I was pretty sure I was in the running for Cinderella. But Miss Alicia told us we'd have to wait until the next morning to find out.

Paterson had watched some of the audition and was waiting for Joey and me in the audience. "Hey, guys, you looked like you were made to dance those parts."

I was getting ready to answer when I noticed Gray coming up behind Paterson. I smiled and tried to look casual, as if it was perfectly natural for him to have come.

But my stomach was fluttering almost as much as it had while I was waiting for my turn to dance.

Gray looked at Joey and me and smiled. "You were both great," he said. "It's really amazing how much energy you guys expend. You must get really hungry. . . ."

Just when I thought Gray was going to suggest we all go out for something to eat, Melissa appeared out of nowhere, like a vampire. "Yes," she chimed in, "I'm starving." She turned to Gray. "Do you want to go to Antonio's? Ivy and I are getting pizza."

Gray looked at Joey and me. "Are you guys going?"

Joey and I shook our heads.

When she could see Gray hesitating, Melissa looked at me. "C'mon, KC, you don't have to get pizza. You can get a salad if you want."

"Why wouldn't she get pizza?" Joey asked, puzzled. I hadn't had a chance to tell him what happened earlier in the day.

I didn't want to confront her with Gray there, but I wanted to stop the rumor right then. "Melissa has this idea that I'm bulimic," I said. "And she told the guidance counselor, who called me in today—coincidentally, right before auditions."

"Well," Joey said, glaring at Melissa, "if that isn't the anorexic calling the ballerina bulimic? You're even more of a bitch than I thought."

Paterson chimed in. "And it's too bad your little plan didn't work. Today Kayla danced better than you'll ever dance—even in your dreams."

Melissa gasped. "I can't believe you'd think I had some kind of plan. I was only trying to help. I was really concerned about you," she said, turning toward me. "I guess you just don't appreciate it."

I looked her straight in the eyes. "Excuse me while I go barf."

She did half a *pirouette* and marched off.

Gray shrugged. "That was weird, huh?"

"You don't even *know*," I said.

"I hate to break up the party, but I've got work to do," Paterson said. "Are you guys ready?"

"Uh, sure." I was so anxious about the results of the audition, I didn't care that I had missed a great opportunity to hang out with Gray. All I could think about was seeing my name on the list the next morning.

Chapter 4

I got to the kitchen just in time to watch Paterson pour Froot Loops and milk into a bowl. "Pleeease," I said. "Can't you have a granola bar in the car, just this once?" She doesn't even like Froot Loops. She just finds them more aesthetically pleasing than other breakfast foods.

Mom looked up from the newspaper. "What's the hurry?"

I threw my backpack onto an empty chair. "Doesn't anyone in this family care about what part I get?"

Paterson shoveled a spoonful of pink and orange Os into her mouth. "You're not going to get a better part if we get there quicker. It's already been determined, like the tides."

"The tides," I yelled. "*What* are you talking about?"

"You know," my mother said, "the tides are controlled by the moon."

Normally I liked my mother's hands-off policy when it came to stage mothering, but this was too much. "Why are the two of you talking about moons and tides when my whole future is hanging in the balance here?"

"Sweetie, it's not your whole future," my mother said. "It only seems like it now. I'm sure you'll get a great part, anyway. You deserve it."

"You certainly do," my father joined in from the hall. "You've paid your dues. That ought to account for something." My dad was big on the idea that certain behaviors yielded certain results. Do something good, get something good in return. It was a philosophy that didn't always work in the dance world, but in the dad world it was sometimes comforting.

"Thanks," I said. "Now please, can we go to school?"

Paterson swallowed her last mouthful and put the bowl in the sink. As she grabbed the sponge, Mom took it from her. "Go," she said, "before your sister explodes." Then she turned to me. "You can tell us all about it tonight. We'll celebrate over dinner."

I got my stuff and followed Paterson out the door. "I hope there'll be something to celebrate."

A huge crowd had already formed around the small piece of paper tacked up on the door of the dance studio. Those closest to the list let out noises that alternated between groans and squeals of delight. Behind them another group stood on their toes and jumped up and down to read the list over everyone else's heads. I joined the jumpers but couldn't see a thing—the writing was way too small.

After my third jump, Lourdes squeezed her way out of the crowd. A few of the freshman dancers trailed behind her shouting, "Congratulations!"

I turned and smiled at her. "Cinderella?" I said, feeling a pang of disappointment.

She smiled.

"If it couldn't be me, you'd be my next choice," I said. I really meant it too.

"Thanks," Lourdes said, "I'm glad you feel that way because . . . you're my *understudy*," she screamed. "We'll be working together to learn the part."

"Oh my God!" I threw my arms around Lourdes and hugged her. "That's so cool."

"Hey, what's with the girl-on-girl action?" The voice behind us was unmistakably Joey's.

Lourdes quickly broke away from me and performed a deep curtsey toward him. "My prince has come," she said.

Joey, who's normally cool about these things, jumped up and grabbed both of us. "Yes!" he yelled.

"Did you see what my real part is?" I shouted to Lourdes over the noise. I figured if I was Cinderella's understudy, I was sure to get one of the four solo parts—Summer, Winter, Spring, or Fall.

"I don't know," she said. "After I saw who got Cinderella and the prince, I pushed my way out of there. I was getting squished. I guess you'll have to go in." She pointed to the blob of dancers still gathered around the list.

All I could see were the backs of everyone's heads. I inched forward, my heart pounding. People began to spread out as I made my way toward the front. Understudy for Cinderella was definitely up there on the ballet food chain. I couldn't wait to find out my real part. Finally I could see over the few heads in front of me. There it was—my name in parentheses next to where it said "Cinderella: Lourdes Castillo." My eyes trailed down the list looking for another sighting of my name. Winter, no—that one went to Melissa. Summer, no—that one was Ivy. Well, there were always Spring and Fall. But my name wasn't next to those, either. I continued down the list. I couldn't help but snicker when I saw Devin was playing the stepmother. Immediately after that, like instant karma or something, I saw my own name. It was next to the word *stepsister*, which suddenly seemed like the most disgusting word in the entire English language. Stepsister. How could I be a stepsister? I was Cinderella's understudy. If I was good enough for that, why wasn't I good enough for a solo? It didn't make sense.

I was still trying to comprehend it all when the first bell rang. As the crowd thinned out, a voice chimed, "Congratulations on the understudy role." It was Ivy, and she was standing next to Melissa.

"Thanks," I mumbled. "You guys, too."

"You know Lourdes has never missed a class," Melissa said. "She hasn't been sick in three years."

"Maybe I should have been your understudy," I shot back. "You're starting to look a little sick."

Melissa smiled her famous fake smile. "Maybe you'll luck out and Lourdes will break her ankle."

I glared at her, then spun around and started toward homeroom. This time I really did want to barf, not because of Melissa's nastiness, but because of my own. A part of me did want Lourdes to get just a little bit sick. What was the point in learning the part of Cinderella if all I was going to do in the whole ballet was some caricature part? Not only that—I wasn't just a stepsister, I was an *ugly* stepsister.

I went through most of the morning trying to concentrate on things like variables and the scientific revolution, but all I could think about was the ballet. I kept picturing myself in red lipstick, painted up to my nostrils, camping it up next to Devin and some poor freshman who got to be the other ugly stepsister. It wasn't so bad, though, when you were a freshman. It was actually a big deal to get any part besides dancing in the corps. But as a junior, and as one of the best dancers in the advanced class, it was something else entirely. It was something . . . incomprehensible.

I was still in a daze when my name blared from the PA system once again in fifth period. I was ready to stand up and scream, "I am *not* bulimic!" when I realized I wasn't being sent to Ms. Marone again. This time it was Miss Alicia who wanted to see me.

For a second time, I packed up my books and left English lit before it was over. Ms. Halstrom gave me a funny smile and waved. By now she probably had a whole novel about me written in her head: *A seemingly innocent ballerina with large breasts has a secret life in a bizarre underworld of danger and deceit.* Maybe it wasn't that far from the truth—especially with my newfound resentment against people I actually liked.

I wasn't sure why Miss Alicia would call me out of

class. Either she had talked to Ms. Marone and was volunteering to help me with my supposed bulimia, or it was about the ballet. I hoped it was the latter. I hoped she was going to tell me it was all a mistake, that some typist had screwed up and put my name in the wrong spot.

Miss Alicia was blocking out some steps to a waltz when I approached the studio. She waved me in and positioned two chairs toward each other. "Sit down," she said. "I wanted to talk about something before class."

Before she could say another word, I blurted out, "I'm not bulimic, if that's what this is about."

Miss Alicia wrinkled her brow. "No, why would I think you're bulimic?"

"No reason," I answered quickly. "What was it you wanted to talk about?"

She rested her ankle on the opposite knee and pointed her toe. "It's about the ballet. I'm sure you were wondering about your part?"

"Umm, no . . . uh . . . well, maybe." I wasn't sure what I was supposed to say. I didn't want to seem like I was questioning her judgment about the part or about what I was feeling.

"You have a right to wonder," she said.

My arms, which had been crossed tightly over my chest, dropped to the seat of the chair. "I do?"

Miss Alicia held onto the arch of her foot. "Of course. You know you deserved a better part, but you also know it wasn't my decision."

She had told us earlier that Timm with two *em*s would have the last word. Suddenly I wanted to rip one of those *em*s off his name and strangle him with it.

"Timm agreed with me that you were a beautiful dancer, perhaps the strongest female in the class when it comes to technique."

Maybe I'd let Timm keep his other *em* after all.

"But he did have some concerns." Miss Alicia pulled her foot closer to her. "He was concerned about your . . . uh, your . . . proportions."

My mouth dropped open. "My proportions?"

"Yes, he feels that they're a . . . how did he put it? A distraction."

"A distraction?" I knew I sounded like an echo, but I couldn't think of any other reply at first. I was sick of talking in euphemisms. Finally I blurted it out. "You mean I got this crummy stepsister role because of my boobs?"

Miss Alicia didn't even bother with her "no small parts" speech. She lowered her eyes. "Timm says that he can't choreograph for breasts the size of yours. In his words, 'It's like they have a mind of their own.' "

My teeth clenched. At least it wasn't because of my

dancing. But it was almost worse. I could improve my dancing. What could I do with my breasts? Timm had said it all. No amount of training would get them moving with the music.

Miss Alicia continued. "I tried to reason with him and explain how you've been such a wonderful student all these years and how you deserve a moment to shine. That's when he agreed you could be Cinderella's understudy."

"But Lourdes has never even missed a class, let alone a performance," I said, realizing I sounded resentful of her good health.

Miss Alicia looked down. "I know, and I'm sorry."

Suddenly the studio didn't seem so comforting anymore. The smell of rosin and old ballet shoes was making me queasy. "I guess you did the best you could." I started to leave.

Miss Alicia reached for my arm. "There's something else I'd like to talk to you about."

I wondered what was left to say. Anything short of a plot to bump off Timm wasn't going to change my mood.

"You know," Miss Alicia continued, "if you want to be a ballerina, you're going to run into a lot of Timms."

I imagined a row of cardboard guys with thinning hair—and me with a rubber dart gun, shooting them all down. "What do you mean?" I said.

"The ballet world is a tough one. In order to compete,

it's not enough just to be good. You've got to look the part."

I was getting angry. "Well, I guess we've already established that I don't."

Miss Alicia looked down at her foot. "I'm sorry, I don't mean to belabor the point. What I'm trying to say is: Have you ever thought of surgery?"

"Surgery?" I wondered how long I could go, just repeating the last word of everyone else's sentences.

"Yes," Miss Alicia said. "Breast reduction surgery."

I could feel a lump rising in my throat, and my breasts began to feel even bigger than they usually did. "But I wear three bras to class, isn't that enough?"

Miss Alicia ignored my question. "The surgery is very safe. I know someone who's had it for medical reasons—back problems. If you decide you want to look into it, I could get you the doctor's name."

I thanked Miss Alicia for the information and told her I needed to get ready for class.

"Think about it," she said as I walked toward the dressing room. My eyes burned. But I was too angry to cry. It wasn't as if I didn't *know* my boobs were big. Or that surgery like that existed. But I was only sixteen. Wasn't that something you did when you were older—after you'd nursed a couple of babies and your boobs were down to your knees?

I rushed out of the dressing room after class and headed toward the art room. I didn't want to hear any more stupid congratulations on getting the understudy role. By now everyone had to know it was a pity part—my real part was one usually played by a man with oversized feet, hamming it up in drag.

"Hey, wait up," Joey yelled. He was the only one I'd stop for. "What's wrong?"

"Nothing," I answered bitterly. "Nothing a little breast surgery couldn't cure."

"What?" came a voice from behind me.

Just what I needed—a dose of Devin, my new "mother."

"Hey, everyone," he yelled. "Kayla's going to have her rack whacked." He turned to me. "Say it isn't so. I won't have anything to look at during *grands jetés* anymore."

I squeezed my bio book to my chest and felt my face flush. Joey grabbed my elbow and we bolted down the hall together. "Go try on your tutu!" he yelled back at Devin.

"That was kind of lame," I whispered.

"Yeah," he said. "I know, but I figured I had to defend your honor."

I looked down at my chest. "It's not my honor that's in jeopardy."

"I can't believe she even suggested it to you," Paterson said. She stopped work on her sketch of Lourdes. "What nerve!"

"I don't think it was her fault," I said. "I think she was just telling me like it is."

"But . . . man," Joey said. "That's cold. It's like telling a guy he's got to have his uh . . . you know, hacked off before he can put on a pair of tights." He shimmied. "It gives me the creeps just thinking about it."

Paterson was quiet while Joey talked, like she was deep in thought. When he finished . . . she announced softly, "You just gave me an idea for my senior art project."

Joey and I looked at each other and shrugged. "What is it?" I asked.

"You'll see," she answered.

"Last time you said that, I ended up naked on your bed," Joey said.

Paterson just smiled.

Chapter 5

By the end of the week, thanks to Devin's big mouth, my boobs were the talk of the school. People I didn't even know were coming up to me between classes and announcing they were proud members of the new Save the Hooters Foundation. Those were the guys.

Most of the girls, however, seemed to have formed their own underground opposition movement—Reduce the Rack. They faked concern and said things like, "I heard what happened. . . ." Then they'd quickly add, "It might be a good idea, though."

The only girl who was violently opposed to the whole thing was Paterson, who insisted on calling it breast amputation surgery, rather than breast reduction surgery.

"It's just like the fairy tale," Paterson said, out of nowhere.

We were at the Steak 'n Shake getting dinner after Friday's rehearsal. I could tell by the tone of her voice that she was back on the subject of the surgery. Lately all roads of conversation seemed to lead directly to my chest. It fit in with her current obsession with feminism, something she had picked up over the summer when we'd gone to New York. While I was dancing, Paterson had taken a women's studies class along with her art courses at one of the universities.

Ordinarily I wouldn't mind Paterson bringing up the subject, but this time Gray was with us. She and Gray shared an art history class, as well as a sketching class, and had become friends. I wasn't sure if this was a good thing or not. Gray was younger than Paterson, and she knew I liked him, but you never could tell what might happen. I hoped maybe he'd been sucking up to Paterson to get to know me better. A little egotistical? I know. But a girl can dream.

"How is what like a fairy tale?" Gray asked.

"The breast amputation," Paterson said. Every time she said it, a searing pain surged through my chest. "It's like *Cinderella*," she continued. "Remember I told you about how in the original fairy tale, the stepsisters cut off their toes so they could fit their feet into the glass slipper? It's the same thing."

Now I was curious. "How?" I said.

Paterson waved a French fry dipped in ketchup as if it were a paintbrush. "The stepsisters were willing to cut their toes off just to marry the prince. All because of some convention that small feet were more acceptable. They were willing to amputate parts of themselves for the sake of what a bunch of ridiculous men thought was beautiful."

I took a sip of Diet Coke. "So what does that have to do with me?"

"Your breasts are like feet," Paterson said.

Joey raised his eyebrows. "Whoa, them's fightin' words. Is this going to end up in a catfight?" He raised his hand like a claw. "Meow!"

A catfight? No. But I wished Paterson would stop talking about my breasts. It wasn't exactly the coolest thing in the world to be sitting in a public place with a guy you've got a major crush on, talking about your boobs. It was *so* not the ideal getting-to-know-you situation.

I looked over to see what Gray's reaction to all of this was. He was pretty absorbed in what Paterson was saying, nodding in all the right places.

"Anyway," Paterson continued. "Your breasts are like the feet, and ballet is like traditional patriarchy. Just like women were supposed to have tiny feet because of male ideals of beauty, you're supposed to have small breasts because of some stupid ballet tradition. Who even knows who started it?"

"She's right," Gray said.

Joey and I both stared at him with our mouths open. It was kind of weird to find someone who agreed with Paterson's feminist tirades. No one at school really took her seriously. Gray Foster was definitely different. And definitely worth getting to know.

"My mom's doing some research about fairy tales, and she gave some lectures," Gray said, a little defensively.

"Finally someone with a brain has come to Farts," Paterson said. "What did she say?"

Gray squirmed in his seat, but continued. "The Little Mermaid—"

Joey jumped in once again. "She doesn't even have feet."

"That's the point," Gray said. "She doesn't, but she's willing to give up the one thing that makes her special in order to have feet so she can be with the sailor."

"What's that?" I asked. I wasn't even faking interest. The way Gray was telling the story, I really wanted to know.

"Her voice," he said.

"But she gets it back," I said. "I saw the movie—the one with the crab and the fish."

Immediately Joey started singing, "Under the sea, under the sea . . ." with a Jamaican accent.

Gray laughed. "That's not the original fairy tale," he said. "In the earlier versions, she sacrifices her tongue—"

Paterson pounded the table like a judge. "Amputation, again."

"She never gets her voice back," Gray continued, "and at the end, the prince marries someone else and the mermaid becomes sea foam."

"They cut off her tongue," Joey said. He took his two fingers and pulled out his tongue, then made scissors with his other hand. "Gwoth."

Suddenly my own tongue felt really big in my mouth.

Gray pushed his empty plate to the side and turned to me. "You know, when I lived in New York, I saw a lot of dance companies with people who had all different bodies. Maybe you could be in one of them. Or maybe you could choreograph your own ballet."

It was quiet for a second, until Joey blurted, "*Booberella*. You could choreograph *and* star in it."

It was kind of a mean thing to say, but you had to

know Joey and our relationship. Besides, it was funny. Once I laughed, everyone else did too.

"You'd be Booberella," Joey went on, "and at midnight, somehow you'd lose your bra while you were running away from the ball."

"Oh," I said. "So then I'll have to go topless in my own ballet."

"That part could be offstage," he said. "Let me finish, I'm on a roll. Instead of the slipper, the prince brings the bra all over the village for all the women to try on."

I was starting to get into it. "And the women try to stuff their bras with tissues and socks and . . ."

"Bed linens," Joey said.

We were laughing so hard, people were starting to stare.

"You know," Gray said. "It's so over the top, it could work. It would really make fun of the original fairy tale."

"You're right," Paterson said. "It would be like a satirical retelling, not like a cartoon or some lame movie like *Pretty Woman*."

"I kind of liked that movie," I said.

Paterson groaned. "Haven't you gotten any of this? The movie tells the same story. That the guy is only going to like you if some fairy godmother—in this case, the hotel manager—arrives and makes you acceptable according to some prescribed patriarchal standard. It's not even anything you have control over."

"Let's not forget," Joey chimed in. "Julia Roberts did have some talent in that movie—she was a hooker. That's how she got the guy."

"Joey, you are so hopeless," Paterson said. She looked at her watch. "Let's get out of here before I pummel you with Kayla's leftover chicken fingers."

As we walked out, Gray turned to me. "You ought to think about a dance company in New York," he said. "You're good enough."

I could tell by his voice that I didn't have to worry about there being anything between him and Paterson.

By the following Monday, my boobs were old news. When I got to the studio to put my dance stuff in the locker room for later, there was a crowd gathered around the door, just like the week before. It felt like déjà vu. For a second I thought maybe Timm with two *em*s had changed his mind and redone the cast list. But I knew that was too good to be true. As I got closer, I could see something red peeking between people's heads. It was a pair of pointe shoes, spray painted the color of blood. Even though it was kind of weird, I couldn't figure out why everyone was so excited about it. That is, until I got closer and read the thin strip of paper streaming out of the shoe: "Dancing in red shoes will kill you."

Chapter 6

As I read the note, which swirled from the pointe shoe like the strip of paper on a Hershey's Kiss, Joey came up behind me.

"What's up?" he said, exaggerating a Prince Charming bow. "Someone lose a slipper?"

We stared at the pointe shoes, hung by their four knotted ribbons, suspended by a single nail. The satin straps were no longer delicate and shiny, but thick with flat red paint, already cracking into puzzle pieces. The shoes had been thoroughly stained, inside and out.

"Is this a joke?" Joey said.

Lourdes was suddenly standing next to us. "If it is, it's not very funny. I'm not sure if anyone's wearing red shoes in the ballet, but it would be pretty creepy if they were."

"Yes, it would," a voice from the crowd announced.

Joey and I spun around to find Melissa standing in third position, hands on her hips and her chin in the air. "The winter costume is always red and white. I might be wearing red shoes in the ballet," she announced. "It figures."

"What figures?" Joey asked.

The crowd that had gathered around the shoes was now focused on us.

"My mother told me to expect jealousy," Melissa said. "After Cinderella, I have the best part in the ballet." She turned toward Lourdes. "Don't worry, that eliminates you." Then she glared straight at me and sneered, "But everyone else is a suspect."

Joey grinned at her. "Who are you, Buffy the Ballerina Slayer?"

Devin, who had been quiet until then, burst out, "Hey, the stepmother's costume is red, too—I saw it on a videotape."

"And here's her sidekick, Dork," Joey added.

Melissa grabbed Devin's arm and marched off. "We'll get to the bottom of this. And when we do, whoever's threatening us better watch out!"

Even Lourdes, who was usually too nice to make fun

of people, laughed with Joey and me as they stalked off together.

"It's the dancing sleuths," Joey yelled after them, "catching criminals with their powerful *pirouettes* and their amazing *arabesques*!"

The first bell rang, and everyone scattered off to homeroom as if the red shoes were just a joke. But for some reason, I had the feeling it was more than that. Even though I knew I might be late for class, I stayed for a minute, wondering who would do something like that and what could the note possibly mean? There were some strange people at Farts, but none of them seemed capable of death threats, let alone actually killing someone.

I examined the slippers for clues, rotating them several times. On the bottom of one shoe, a tiny black mark peeked out from a section of flaking paint. It looked like some kind of symbol, but I couldn't figure out what it was. I checked out the hallways on either side. No one was around, so I peeled a little more of the paint off with my fingernail until a tiny letter *E* appeared.

I twirled the other slipper and scratched like a cat on the leather sole. The back of my neck tingled as that old saying about curiosity and cats sounded in my mind. And even though I pretty much knew what I was looking for, the tingling shimmied down my spine and performed a straddle split to the backs of my knees when I saw the second marking.

For years I had watched her painstakingly inscribe those letters on the soles of fresh pointe shoes—the meticulously drawn *M* on one and the equally self-conscious *E* printed on the other.

Melissa Edwards. What was she up to this time?

I looked around to find someone, anyone, who would recognize the initials and be a witness. But everyone had rushed off to class. I thought about bringing the shoes to the principal's office, but there was no proof that Melissa had written those letters. What did the principal know about Melissa's narcissism and her lifelong habit of marking her territory with ME, ME, ME printed in block letters? It was just my word, which might not be too reliable these days, thanks to Melissa and Ivy and their bulimia blabber.

The second bell was about to ring any minute. Ms. Powers, my European history teacher, was also my homeroom teacher. She wouldn't have understood that I was trying to catch a criminal. She was hung up on Napoleon and couldn't understand why the rest of us didn't share her passionate interest in his exploits. I'd get a lecture ten minutes long on tardiness, and somehow she'd manage to throw in a story linking Napoleon's initial success to his ability to show up on time. I had no choice but to rush off, taking my suspicions with me.

I hoped Miss Alicia would get to the studio soon and find the shoes before word got to the main office. Maybe she would look at the soles and recognize the initials.

All morning I waited for an announcement over the loudspeaker about the shoes. What I was really hoping to hear was Melissa's name with a request to go to the principal's office. But I never heard either of those things. It was as if nothing had happened.

My mind raced with possible reasons why Melissa would do something so weird. What was up with the red shoes? And why would she announce that *she* might be wearing red shoes in the ballet? Even though I wouldn't put anything past her, death threats against herself was a little too schizo, even for Melissa. Unless . . . she wanted it to look like someone else was threatening her. Maybe that was what that dancing detective act was all about. But why go through all that trouble just to make it look like someone had it in for you?

I got my answer in third period.

By then everyone had heard about the shoes. And like that game Telephone, the story had become greatly exaggerated.

Third period is calculus for me. I'm not bragging, but hardly any dancers are that far in math by junior year. It has to do with the amount of time we spend at the stu-

dio and that right brain, left brain thing. I just happen
to be good in math. In fact, most of the people in the
class are computer graphics geeks. They don't know
much about the dance department, or any other department for that matter. If you're not talking web design or
Star Trek, they're not interested.

So I was kind of surprised when Donald, the guy
next to me, said, "Hey, did you hear about the psycho in
the dance department?"

"What?" I said. "A psycho?" Wow, I guessed Miss
Alicia had found the shoes and recognized the writing. I
was relieved that Melissa had gotten caught, but I did
think the word *psycho* was a little harsh. She was imma-
ture and mean, but she wasn't all killing-someone-in-the-
shower kind of crazy.

Donald looked at me with wide eyes. "Yeah," he said.
"I heard it's some girl who's pissed because she got the
understudy role of Cinderella. She's threatening to kill
anyone with a better part. Weird, huh?"

I just stared at him. I'm pretty sure my mouth
dropped open too.

I didn't have to think too hard to figure out who could
have started that rumor. I couldn't believe Melissa had
spread it so quickly and that people had bought into it.

"That is totally a lie!" I blurted. "A vicious lie." Then
I noticed a button he was wearing. It pictured an owl.

Where its eyes should have been, huge bare breasts stared out at me. The picture was just ambiguous enough that teachers wouldn't notice. Underneath, in small letters, it read SAVE THE HOOTERS.

"Where did you get that?" I demanded.

Donald put his head down. "One of my friends made it," he mumbled.

"You want to save the hooters?" I said through my teeth. "Tell your friends to stop spreading rumors or I'll rip those buttons off every one of their plaid polyester shirts."

Donald drew away from me. "Okay, okay."

I knew I was risking another trip to the guidance office. This time for uncontrollable rage and anger management.

I was livid for the rest of math class. I wasn't sure if it was because of Donald's stupid button or the ridiculous rumor.

I was beginning to feel as if my breasts were public property, something for people to ponder and make decisions about, even though it was none of their business. And how dare Melissa put up those shoes and then try to pin it on me, especially when she'd gotten a better part than I did. How could she be threatened by my pitiful understudy role? What was Melissa's problem?

By the time advanced ballet class rolled around, the pointe shoes had been removed from the door. I inspected the inside of the studio—the rosin box, the table with Miss Alicia's music, the corner where everyone threw their sweaty towels—but the shoes were nowhere to be seen. Without them, there was no way I was going to convince anyone they belonged to Melissa.

Before *pliés*, Miss Alicia had us sit on the studio floor. We could all guess what was coming.

"As you all know, a pair of pointe shoes and a foolish note were found hanging on the door of the studio this morning." She stood with her right foot in a *tendu* and her hands on her hips. "I'm sure no one in here would do such a thing. . . ."

I stared at Melissa's reflection in the mirror to see if I could detect a trace of guilt. Not one iota. She was either a total sociopath, a great actress, or—and this one was hard to believe—an innocent bystander. She stared at Miss Alicia with the same earnestness as everyone else, the same wide-eyed look that Lourdes wore, as if she were asking who would want to hurt a fellow dancer.

I wasn't fooled by her. Nevertheless, I scanned the rest of the class for suspects. Only the faces of Devin and Ivy deviated from the uniform look of apprehension and boredom. Devin was flexing his calf muscle and measuring the bulge with his fingers, and Ivy appeared to be staring at Miss Alicia's eyebrows. Right then I deemed both of them innocent by reason of inanity.

Miss Alicia continued. "We have all worked very hard this year, and *Cinderella* will be the culmination of our hard work. I'm sure no one wants to ruin this ballet with pranks and tomfoolery."

Joey leaned toward me. "Pranks and Tomfoolery, sounds like a comedy team."

I tried to smile, but all I kept thinking about was seeing those black initials underneath that veneer of red paint.

Miss Alicia continued, ignoring the apathy of her audience. "I'm sure that whoever placed those shoes on the door meant it to be humorous, but I would hope that it doesn't happen again."

Joey leaned in again. "Humorous death threats. Now there's a concept."

This time I whispered back. "Yeah. If you're Hannibal Lecter."

Joey mimicked that creepy slurp Anthony Hopkins did in the movie and whispered, "'I ate his liver with some fava beans and a nice Chianti.'"

Miss Alicia glared at him. "I've heard rumors that some of you believe that you will be wearing red shoes in the ballet."

Melissa and Devin turned to each other and nodded vigorously.

"Let me say that at this point, it is uncertain as to who will be wearing what, so your speculations are unfounded."

Devin raised his hand. "There's a videotape at Blockbuster that shows the whole ballet and what everyone's wearing."

"I'm sure there is," Miss Alicia said. "But that doesn't mean we'll be wearing the same costumes."

Melissa raised her hand. "Didn't Ballet on the Beach do *Cinderella* a couple of years ago? If anyone saw that, they'd know what the costumes look like. Timm said we'd be using the same ones."

"You may be right, Melissa, but we're all friends here and I expect that we will all support each other in this ballet."

Had it been so long that Miss Alicia had forgotten the rivalries that developed when parts were at stake? Did she really buy that "everything is beautiful at the ballet" stuff? Even the people in *A Chorus Line* who sang those words didn't believe them.

I continued to scour the dancers in the studio for any nuance of guilt during barre exercises as well as during leaps across the floor.

Joey was behind me as I waited for my turn to *grand jeté*. I paused for a second before taking off. "I have something to tell you," I whispered. I began the run before my leap.

After his foot gently landed on the wooden floor behind me, Joey whispered, "What?"

Miss Alicia clapped several times. "Let's go. Let's go. We have a lot to do today."

"Tell you later," I whispered as I approached the front of the line again and began my second dash across the floor.

For the rest of class, I watched Melissa's face for clues as she performed the standard center work. Her chin, raised above her long, thin neck, was tilted slightly higher than normal ballet posture. More arrogant than elegant. Her tight bun was stuck to the back of her head like a doorknob. I wanted to pull on it and find out what was inside that twisted little mind of hers.

I had to find out if anyone had noticed the initials on the bottoms of the shoes. I rehearsed what I was going to say to Miss Alicia while I watched the other groups perform the combination of *pirouettes* and *pas de chats*. When we finally finished, I pretended the ribbons on my pointe shoe were tangled in a knot so I'd be the last one in the room.

"Miss Alicia," I said. "I was wondering, umm, what happened to the shoes that were hanging on the door this morning?"

She was struggling to fit a CD into a plastic sleeve. "I'm not sure," she said. "Someone from the main office came and got them. I think they might have been turned over to Ms. Marone, the guidance counselor. Why do you ask?"

For a minute I thought about telling her what I suspected. But then I realized it wouldn't prove anything. Melissa could say the shoes were stolen from her. She could even say *I* stole them from her. I envisioned myself looking more guilty than Melissa was already trying to make me appear.

Miss Alicia shoved the CD into a plastic filing box.

"No reason," I said. "I was just wondering what the big deal was about them."

"I don't think there is any big deal," Miss Alicia said, "I'm sure it's someone's idea of a joke. But I'm glad you came to see me."

What was it this time, I wondered. Did Timm with two *em*s think I needed a nose job, too?

Miss Alicia reached into her drawer and pulled out a business card. "This is the doctor I told you about. I've heard good things about him. Another friend of mine went to him for the opposite problem, and she was very happy with the results."

I wrapped my fingers around the card without looking at it. "Thanks," I said. I hadn't really thought of my breasts as "problem breasts." It made them sound like children who wouldn't behave. Miss Alicia's friend must have thought her breasts were too small. That didn't seem to qualify as a full-fledged "problem" to me. Few fulfilling careers required cantaloupe boobs. And even if they did, you could always wear a Wonderbra. Victoria's Secret had yet to make an undergarment that could hide eight pounds of flesh. I looked down. No bra was going to keep these babies a secret. And those tips for the full-figured girl in the magazines. Please. Even NASA couldn't design a tank suit to camouflage my proportions.

When I got to the art room, Paterson was working on a new sketch of a girl's face. Joey was watching intently until he heard me come in. "Where were you?" he said. "I waited for you by the girl's dressing room, but you never came out. And speaking of coming out, I don't think Gray will be any time soon—he asked me yesterday if you had a boyfriend."

I dropped my dance bag on the floor, nearly missing my toe. "Are you serious?"

"As a bunion."

"Why didn't you tell me this morning?"

"Oh, you mean during the killer pointe shoe fiasco?"

"You're right," I said. "I guess death threats should take precedence over prospective boyfriends."

Paterson stopped sketching. "Death threats?"

"You didn't hear?" I said.

"All I heard was something about red shoes."

Joey slid a painting of big purple flowers down one of the art tables and hoisted himself up, his feet dangling. "Where have you been all day?"

"In here most of the time," Paterson said. "Old Etch A Sketch gave me a pass so I could work on my project." Etch A Sketch was Paterson's nickname for Mr. Walker, one of the art teachers whose work seemed to show a passion for straight lines, something Paterson didn't find particularly interesting.

"It's a little more than a pair of shoes," I said. "No matter what Miss Alicia thinks. That's what I was trying to tell you in class, Joey."

Paterson stopped sketching. "You're right."

For a second I thought maybe she knew something and could shed light on what was going on. Until she added, "They're phallic symbols."

I groaned. I was not up for a psychological discussion. I was being framed, and soon everyone was going to know it.

Joey laughed. "To paraphrase Freud, sometimes a pointe shoe is just a pointe shoe."

"I'm serious," I said. "I think Melissa's trying to set me up. This kid in my calculus class told me he heard a rumor that the shoes were put up by a psycho who got the understudy role of Cinderella."

Paterson was drawing a large open mouth on the girl in the picture. "No one's going to believe you would do something like that."

"She's right," Joey said. "Melissa's the only person who would be capable of that kind of thing, and everyone knows it."

I wasn't sure if I could believe them or not. The ballet people knew about Melissa, but the rest of the school didn't. What if she was able to convince everyone else that *she* was the victim?

"I forgot to tell you the most important part," I said. "I looked at the bottom of the shoes and peeled some of the paint off. Melissa's initials were printed on the soles."

"Whoa," Joey said. "She *is* a psycho."

Paterson dropped her pencil. "Wait a minute. You mean they're her shoes? She painted them, put them up there with a death threat, and now she's trying to pin it on you?"

Joey shook his head. "That is so wrong. Did anyone else see the initials?"

"No," I said. "That's the problem. And now who knows where the shoes are."

Paterson pulled the cover down on her sketch pad and packed up her pencils. "I don't think people would

78

believe you'd do a thing like that."

Joey jumped down from the art table. "And if they do, you can always teach ballet to your fellow inmates at the women's detention center."

I hit him with my backpack as we walked out.

That night when I pulled my dirty leotard and tights out of my dance bag, I found the card Miss Alicia had given me crumpled up and stuck inside my pointe shoe. I smoothed it out and looked at it. DR. ANDERSEN MARLOWE, PLASTIC SURGEON.

Marlowe, I thought, like Marlo Thomas. I remembered reading in one of Paterson's books about the controversy the actress caused in the old show *That Girl* when she didn't wear a bra and her boobs bounced all over the television screen. What the hell was everybody's thing with breasts?

I put the card on my dresser next to my hairspray. I knew what Paterson would say about Dr. Marlowe.

I stuffed clean dance clothes into the bag and thought about how much had happened that day. My head was swirling with thoughts of death threats and plastic surgeons. Whatever happened to sugarplums and fairies?

I'd almost forgotten about Gray Foster. If anything could take my mind off my problems, it was him. As I crawled into bed, I thought about what Joey had said. Gray had to be interested in me—why else would he care if I had a boyfriend? I closed my eyes and tried to picture Gray's face. But those stupid red pointe shoes kept floating in front of it.

Chapter 7

"Wake up. Wake up," a voice commanded. I opened my eyes to find Paterson standing next to my bed with a book and a videotape in one hand and a bowl of popcorn in the other.

I squinted at her. "What are you doing, waking me up so early on Saturday?"

"It's almost noon," she said. "I've already been to the library and back."

I rubbed my eyes and sat up. "What for?"

She held up the book and tape. "Clues," she said.

"Clues? Who are you, Nancy Drew?" I hadn't intended the pun, but when I realized what I'd said, I laughed and added, "Get it? Drew. You're an artist?"

Paterson ignored me. "I thought you'd be a little more concerned about psycho ballerina and her killer pointe shoes." She pulled the covers off me. "C'mon, we've got work to do."

I didn't think Paterson had taken me seriously when I'd told her about Melissa's initials being on the shoes. It had been almost a week since the whole red shoes fiasco. And, more importantly, three days since I'd last run into Gray before rehearsal. We didn't have any classes together, so there was no chance of seeing him during school. I'd fantasized about running into him somehow over the weekend, but I had no idea where he lived or hung out.

Instead, I was going to spend my Saturday playing detective with Paterson. I made my way to the bathroom, getting a whiff of popcorn and turning up my nose as I passed her.

"I just popped it in the microwave," Paterson said, following me to the bathroom. "It's low fat. You'll be glad we have it during the movie."

"What is this movie, anyway?"

Paterson held up the box.

I brought it close to my eyes. "*The Red Shoes*—I've heard of that somewhere."

"It's a classic," Paterson said, "from nineteen forty-eight."

After I put my contact lenses in, I got a better look at the front cover. Under a picture of a ballerina, the caption read: BETWEEN HER ART AND HER DREAMS WAS HER HEART. I looked up at Paterson. "Just like me," I said, "except between my art and my dreams are my boobs."

"Hold that thought," Paterson said. "It might be a clue."

I squeezed a mint-green snake onto my toothbrush. "Are you kidding?"

"No," she said. "Whoever put up those shoes, whether it's Melissa or not, they had to know something about the fairy tale, the movie, or both."

"What fairy tale?" I asked through a mouthful of toothpaste.

"*The Red Shoes*," Paterson said with impatience. She held up a children's book that pictured a girl wearing a huge white dress and red pointe shoes. "Our psycho picked red shoes for a reason. The note didn't say, 'Dancing in pink shoes will kill you,' or 'Dancing in puce shoes will kill you.'"

"Puce?" I said, spitting into the sink.

"It's a dark red," Paterson said. "But it's all beside the point. The fairy tale and the movie have to be the keys."

I didn't have the energy to argue with her. By the time she fed the tape into the VCR and pressed PLAY, I was already on the couch with a mouthful of popcorn.

"Why don't we call Joey to come watch it with us?"

"Already called this morning. He had something to do."

What could Joey have to do on a Saturday that didn't involve us? I vowed never to forgive him for making me sit here and watch this with Paterson, who seemed to have gone all *Murder She Wrote* on me.

I couldn't believe she was making me watch this. It was the slowest movie I'd ever seen. Normally, I don't like car chases, but this film practically cried out for one. Aside from the fact that the movie showed a bunch of laughable close-ups with melodramatic music, the thing that was really noticeable was the ballerinas' bodies and technique.

"Look at those *arabesques*," I said. "They're barely at ninety degrees."

"It's just like athletes," Paterson said. "Years ago people thought it was impossible to break a four-minute mile, then some guy in the fifties did it and, suddenly, thousands of people were doing it. The bar's always rising."

"That's for sure," I said. "Even with the bodies." I pointed to the screen. "A few of those ballerinas have got some major thighage going on. What's up with that?"

"It's like those art books with the rotund women you were looking at," Paterson said. "It's all cultural. Once society accepts something, it becomes the norm."

Just as I reached for some more popcorn and sank back into the leather cushion, the doorbell rang. Paterson hit the pause button and I galloped to the door. Even a Jehovah's Witness would have provided welcome relief.

"Hey," I said, relieved to find Joey standing there. "I thought you had something to do."

He walked by me and made his way to the popcorn. "Finished early," he said.

"Lucky you," I answered. "You're just in time to join the Sleuth Sisters and their search for clues in the great Red Shoe Riddle. But the real mystery is why we're watching this boring movie."

"Okay, that's enough," Paterson said, punching the play button.

Joey took off his sneakers and sat cross-legged on the couch next to me. For the next hour, we talked in sign language and made faces behind Paterson's head. Then, all of a sudden, something caught our attention—a big blowup between the main ballerina's husband and the ballet director. They were making her choose between them.

"Why can't she have both?" I said.

"Nineteen forty-eight, remember?" Paterson said. "A good wife doesn't go traipsing all over the world to dance."

"Why not?" Joey said.

I brought my finger to my lips. "Shhh. It's starting to get good." The dancer had defiantly put on a pair of red pointe shoes and her husband was storming off. It looked like she had chosen ballet over him. "Yay," I said. "He wasn't even cute."

"Not even a two," Joey said. "Where did they get these guys?"

But then, suddenly, the ballerina was going after the husband, running on pointe in the red shoes, out of the dressing room, out of the theater, onto a balcony, calling after him, nearing the railing and then . . . *splat*!

"What the—" I cried. But before I could finish, there was her husband next to her and, apparently, she could still speak. In a limp voice she uttered the words: "Take the red shoes off." The husband removed the shoes and put his face near her legs.

"Kiss those bloody feet," Joey said as the husband put his lips on the shredded and stained tights.

For a minute I thought the ballerina was going to survive, but then she abruptly turned her face, closed her eyes, then . . . Boom. Dead. "That was the worst ending I've ever seen," I said. "Why didn't she stop when she got to the railing?"

"Did she kill herself?" Joey said.

Paterson turned around. "It was the red shoes."

"That's crazy," I said. "How could the shoes kill her?"

Paterson picked up the book she'd had earlier. "It's like the fairy tale," she said, leafing through the pages.

"What's that all about?" Joey asked.

"A little girl who disobeys the woman who adopted her by wearing red shoes."

I sat up and adjusted my bra. "What's wrong with red shoes?"

"Something about vanity," Paterson said. "Anyway, she wears the shoes and then, somehow, they get stuck to her feet and she can't stop dancing in them. She dances herself into such a frenzy that she has to have her feet cut off to stop."

"That's pretty harsh," Joey said. "Then what happens?"

Paterson looked at the book. "First she gets wooden feet, then she goes to heaven."

"Isn't there some religious belief that someday your soul will be reunited in heaven with a perfect body?" I said.

"Sounds familiar," Paterson said. "But whose idea of perfection are we talking about?"

"I don't know, but I was kind of hoping I could spend eternity in a size thirty-four B Victoria's Secret bra instead of one like this." I pulled a two-inch-thick bra strap out from under my T-shirt.

Paterson laughed. "Maybe God loves your boobs. Maybe *She* thinks they're perfect and wants you to keep them forever."

"That's sick," I said.

"You know you're probably going to hell for that, Paterson," Joey added.

"It's not as bad as a death threat," Paterson said. "Remember, that's what we're here for—to figure out what's going on."

"What?" Joey said.

"I guess I didn't really explain it all. Paterson thinks the red shoes at school have something to do with the movie or the fairy tale."

Joey just laughed.

Paterson popped the videotape out and slid it into the container. "What's so funny?"

"I don't know," he said. "Wooden feet? Homicidal pointe shoes?"

"Joey's right," I said. "Besides, who in the dance program would even know about this movie—or the fairy tale. Everyone's so into ballet. I'm telling you, Melissa's initials were on the backs of those shoes, and she's practically illiterate."

"Do you think she did it to frame you? To make it look like you're the one with the problem?" Paterson asked.

"It wouldn't be the first time," I said, remembering a performance when she stole Ivy's sequined sash and stuck it in my dance bag.

"But why red shoes?" Paterson said. "Is that what she's wearing in the ballet?"

"I don't know," I said. "But she seems to think it's common knowledge that red shoes go with her costume. Maybe there's a catalog somewhere—" My thoughts were interrupted by the ringing phone.

I leaned over to pick it up and immediately felt a tingling sensation in the backs of my knees when I heard the voice at the other end. "Hey guys," I yelled, "it's Gray." I wasn't sure why I'd announced it to everyone, but I was so surprised to hear his voice on the other end of the line that it was the first thing that came out of mouth. He must've had to do some digging to get our phone number because it wasn't listed. Score one for the ugly stepsister!

"Hey, Gray," Paterson shouted.

"Gray, what's up?" Joey added in a loud voice.

Then Joey grabbed Paterson and pretended to be Gray, making out with me. He ran his hands along Paterson's back and murmured, "Oh, Kayla, you're such a great dancer. Will you go out with me?"

I rolled my eyes and tried to keep my mind on what Gray was saying. "He wants to know if we can go to his mother's poetry reading next Saturday," I reported to Paterson and Joey.

Gray cleared his throat. "Actually," he said. "I was wondering if *you* would want to go."

My stomach fluttered like the arms of the dying bird in Swan Lake. This was more than I'd hoped for. Not a foursome or a casual meeting in school. A real date. Who cared if it was to go see his mother read her poetry? It was still a date.

I covered the mouthpiece and whispered to Paterson and Joey, "He meant just *me*."

Paterson mouthed the word *dork* and then yelled loudly, "Can't—got to work on my art project."

Joey quickly added in a booming voice, "I've got to wash my jockstrap that night."

Paterson pretended to knee him in the crotch.

"What did he say?" Gray asked.

"Nothing," I said. "But I'd love to go to your mom's reading. What kind of poetry does she write?"

It was difficult to pay attention to the answer with Paterson falling all over Joey, whispering, "I love poetry. I've read *The Cat in the Hat* at least ten times. . . ."

I thought I heard Gray say something about mythology, but I wasn't sure. Paterson was whispering something about Dr. Seuss's use of metaphor in *There's a Wocket in my Pocket.*

I finally decided there was no way I was going to have an intelligent conversation while Joey and Paterson were performing their little skit. I told Gray we'd talk more in school on Monday and hung up.

I grabbed a handful of popcorn. "Thanks a lot, you guys."

Then I threw the popcorn up in the air and began waving my arms and skipping around, screaming, "I've got a date! I've got a date!"

Joey flopped onto the couch. "This is so pathetic," he said. "We're at our sexual peak and when one of us finally gets a date, it's popcorn-throwing time."

Paterson shoved him. "We don't need dates. We have art."

"Art?" Joey said. "Sounds like a short fat guy with a receding hairline."

"You can afford to make jokes," Paterson said. "But I've got a project to work on. Etch A Sketch wants to see the preliminary drawings this week." Her words trailed off as she headed toward her room.

I turned to Joey. "So where were you this morning?"

He shrugged. "Nowhere."

"Do you want to help me plan for my date?"

Joey laughed. "Not really."

"Well then, do you want some lunch?"

He shook his head. "I've got some homework to

do. I think I'll take off."

"Since when do you do homework?" I yelled as he was walking out the door.

I thought it was strange that he didn't stay for lunch. And that he was going home to do work—especially since he had a severe case of senioritis. But it didn't matter. I had a date with Gray Foster!

ew ballet would look like. Even more so now,
he circumstances. I sat between Joey and Lourdes
Alicia ripped the tape off the first box. I had an
feeling in my stomach, remembering what Devin
lissa had said a while ago about being the only
o could possibly wear red shoes. I was afraid if
was right, the rumors might start all over again.
s time we had Officer Ballanchine just waiting to
o.
d my breath as Miss Alicia pulled out the first
—a long pink skirt attached to a satin camisole
llective "Ohhhhhhh" floated across the stage.
Alicia pulled out about fifteen more of the same
from the box as the guys mimicked us in high-
oices. The girls in the corps came up one at a
held the costumes in front of themselves. I was
didn't have to fit my boobs into one of those
s.
came the soloists. Ivy's costume was a pale yel-
with white sequins on the top. Melissa's was all
silver sequins. I couldn't see red shoes going
r of those costumes. Or any of the others in
Or the next two boxes.
time we got to box number four, Joey, Devin,
nd I were practically on top of Miss Alicia.
ume was first—thick gray tights, a white satin

Chapter 8

By the time Paterson and I got to Farts on
Monday, the whole school was in an uproar.
Three more pairs of red pointe shoes had popped
up. This time with no notes. Still, everyone knew what
they meant. A line like "Dancing in red shoes will kill
you" isn't something you're likely to forget. And somehow, without the written threat it was even creepier, sort
of like the scary music they play in horror movies when
someone's walking down a dark hallway.

When the first pair of shoes appeared, the administration had tried a hands-off policy, chalking it up to a
one-time only prank. After a day or two, even the
rumors about the rivalries in the dance department—the

false ones that Melissa started—eventually died down. But this time the administration couldn't ignore it. The shoes had been posted in other departments—outside the art studio, on the door of the orchestra room, and in the hall between the drama department and the auditorium. Even though they were removed immediately, word of their appearance flew like sweat during a double *pirouette*.

It was obvious that those in charge of the school had no idea how to handle the whole thing. Throughout the week they tried various tactics. Every afternoon Principal Kovac got on the loudspeaker and announced that he was not a principal who fooled around. This always brought on loud snickering throughout each class. It was widely rumored that Mr. Kovac and the tenth-grade guidance counselor, Ms. Strickland, did, indeed, fool around, although no one could quite figure out why. She was in her thirties and fairly attractive. He was about twenty years older, short, balding, duck footed, and married. The only thing he seemed to have going for him was that he could do whatever he wanted around the school, including make lame announcements every afternoon. Even some of the teachers had to stifle a laugh when he'd make one of his grand pronouncements about how he was going to "get to the bottom of these sinister shoes that threatened to stomp

all over the good name of Florida Arts

After a couple of days, a new No B put into effect. Everyone had to bring plastic bags so teachers could see if any a weapon—or another pair of lethal That was especially fun for me, trying tard and tights around my two giant e would see. After two days of torn plas in excuses as to why no one had the the No Backpack rule was rescinded.

Because of the obvious connection mainly on the dance department. Th cer had started spending a lot of ti classes and rehearsals. He was a y though he always wore a stern exp sure it wasn't exactly a hardship for of girls in leotards and tights. Som auditorium and watch from the a he'd swagger backstage as if he we thing.

"Who does he think he is?" Jo "Balanchine?"

Other than Joey's sarcasm, thi until that Friday—when the cost

We all crowded around the stage. It was always a big event to

shirt, and a navy vest with gold trim.

He held the shirt up to his chest.

"Very princely," I said.

Devin took his head out of the box. "Don't you mean queenly?"

"Is that any way for a stepmother to talk?" Joey said as he folded the shirt back up.

Devin's face got red. "Don't you have a 'We're queer, we're here, get used to it' rally to go to?"

Joey grinned. Whenever Devin resorted to gay insults, it was clear he was feeling threatened. "Don't you have an 'I'm straight, I'm great, I'm a loser' rally to go to?"

By then everyone was laughing hysterically, Miss Alicia was clapping like mad to get our attention, and Officer B. had made his way from the wings to break up what he seemed to think was the beginning of a brawl, rather than the usual banter between Joey and Devin.

When things finally calmed down, Miss Alicia pulled out Cinderella's two costumes. The first was a long gray skirt with an apron and a white peasant blouse. I figured I could fit into that in the off chance that I'd have to step in for Lourdes. But when Cinderella's ball costume was revealed, I knew my understudy career was over. The flowing gold skirt was fine. But the minuscule top with the gold sequins looked like it would have fit a Barbie doll—a real one, not a life-size doll that would, by the way, have boobs almost as big as mine if it were blown up proportionately. Neither real-life Barbie nor I would ever fit into that costume. If anything were to happen to Lourdes at the last minute, I'd need about three extra yards of fabric to insert in the side seams. At that moment I prayed Lourdes would remain healthy throughout the performances.

The last three costumes were for the stepmother and ugly stepsisters—Devin, me, and a freshman named Karen. All three looked like old-fashioned dresses with pinafores and petticoats. Devin took the dress and folded it quickly. I almost felt sorry for him.

Miss Alicia dragged one of the boxes to the side of the stage. Officer B. took another one. "At least he's good for something," Joey whispered.

"Now I want you all to put these costumes in a safe place before we rehearse," Miss Alicia said. "Then when you get home, hang them up to get the wrinkles out. You're all in charge of your own costumes, so take good care of them."

Melissa, who had been strangely quiet during the whole thing, raised her hand. "What about our shoes?" she said, her eyes darting toward mine.

"Oh, I almost forgot," Miss Alicia said, gesturing toward the wings. "There's a smaller box over there."

Upon the mention of shoes, Officer B. was hot on the trail. He retrieved the box, plopped it in front of Miss Alicia, and stood over it like a sentinel.

Several pairs of pink shoes with names written in marker on the plastic wrapping were distributed first. Then a few pairs of white. I was relieved to see Melissa's name on one of those. A few pairs of black. Then . . .

All I heard was a collective gasp. Miss Alicia had pulled out three pairs of red pointe shoes. She turned the first pair to read the marking on the plastic and called out Karen's name. I knew mine and Devin's names would be next.

Before Miss Alicia got a chance to hand any of us our shoes, Officer B. was suddenly beside me. "I'd like a word with you three," he said in a voice that seemed several octaves lower than it should have been. "And you too, Miss Alicia."

I almost laughed, hearing a big guy like him call her Miss Alicia.

He turned toward her. "Where did this box come from?"

Miss Alicia gestured toward some markings on the cardboard. "From Ballet on the Beach. Timm arranged for the costumes and shoes."

Officer B. folded his arms over his chest. "What about the vee-hicle they were transported in?"

Miss Alicia tucked a loose bobby pin back into her bun. "I brought them over myself."

"Did anyone have prior knowledge as to the color of these ballet slippers?"

Miss Alicia sighed. "I suppose anyone who has ever seen a catalog of costumes suggested for the ballet would know."

Officer B. faced the rest of the dancers who were still on the floor, flexing and stretching. "Has anyone here ever seen a catalog of costumes for *Cinderella*?"

A few people looked up from their exercises. No one raised a hand. I wanted to tell him it was highly unlikely that the perpetrator would admit to seeing a catalog. Geez. Didn't he watch cop shows?

Miss Alicia turned toward him. "May I start my class now?"

Officer B. nodded. "I'd like to speak to these three privately."

"That's fine," she said, "but please don't keep them long. They need to warm up."

Officer B. led us down the stage steps and into the audience seats. He had us sit in the first row while he struck an official-looking stance, his legs apart and feet turned out. He was doing a great second position, but I didn't think he would appreciate the ballet critique.

He looked at me first. Well, actually, he looked at my

boobs first, then up at my eyes. "Do you have any enemies?" he said.

I thought for a minute, wondering if Melissa was
worth mentioning. It was true that her initials were on
that first pair of pointe shoes and she *had* tried to get me
out of the way with that phony bulimia thing, but . . .
when it came right down to it, I didn't think I could
accuse her of anything like murder threats without more
proof. I shook my head no.

Officer B turned to Karen and asked her the same
question.

She shook her whole body no, as if she was shivering.
I was pretty sure Karen was like most of the dancers at
Farts. Her only real enemy was a jumbo-sized bag of
peanut M&M's.

Officer B. then turned to Devin. "How about you?"

Devin hesitated for a few seconds. "N—n—no."

"What about that guy up there—weren't you two
fighting earlier?"

Before Devin answered, he looked toward me. I shot
him a glance that told him he better say no. For a second
I thought Officer B. had seen it. But he was looking at
my boobs again.

Devin shook his head.

Officer B. leaned toward us. "I just want you to know
that I'll be watching out for you three. If you ever think

anyone's following you or if you think your life is in danger, come to me first."

"Okay," we all said in unison.

As we climbed the stairs to the stage, I felt bad for making fun of him. He was just trying to do his job. I guess he felt he had to play a role, just like we did when we were dancing. But did he have to play the role with such a deep voice?

After we rehearsed the ball scene from the ballet, Miss Alicia dismissed us and told a few people that Timm with two *em*s would be rehearsing with them over the weekend to work on choreographing their parts. She didn't say anything about the shoes.

"So what did you say?"

"I told him, no, I didn't think I had any enemies." Joey and I passed by one of the places where a pair of red pointe shoes had been hanging earlier in the week. We looked at the empty spot without saying a word.

Joey seemed like he was getting ready to say something else, but as we got closer to the art room we could hear Paterson's voice ranting in a way I'd never heard.

When we opened the double doors of the room, Paterson was waving her arms and yelling, "How dare they tell us what is art and what isn't!"

I was just about to ask Paterson what the deal was

when I spotted Gray, sitting on a nearby stool. My knees went into an involuntary plié as he turned to me, smiled, and then went back to nodding in agreement with Paterson.

Before she could start up again, Joey yelled out, "Whoa. What's going on?"

Paterson spun toward us so fast I could hear her newly magenta hair slap against her face. "What's going on," she said, "is that my senior art project proposal has been rejected by Principal Kovac and his administration of obedient puppets."

I dropped my backpack on the floor. "That's crazy. Why?"

"They think it's obscene," Paterson said. "I'll tell them what's obscene. Censorship. That's obscene."

I gave Gray a quick smile and turned back toward Paterson. "What do they mean by obscene? What does your art project look like anyway?"

"Yeah," Joey said. "You've been keeping this thing a secret. What's up?"

"Follow me," Paterson said. She walked to a corner of the room where a drop cloth covered an easel holding a huge canvas. She held the edge of the paint-splattered fabric delicately before the unveiling. "It's called 'Tales of Missing Pieces.' I don't care if you don't like it; just tell me it's not obscene."

She jerked her arm over her head and raised the cloth like a curtain on opening night. It whooshed upward and then dropped behind the easel.

Joey and I gasped. Gray, who wasn't surprised at all, had apparently already seen it before we got there.

At the top left corner was a sketch of Lourdes with no foot, except it didn't really look like Lourdes anymore. To the right was a picture of what used to look like me, but without breasts. At the bottom left was a sketch of a girl's face with an open mouth and no tongue. And to the right of that was a foot with some toes missing. But the real shocker was in the middle. It was definitely Joey, but Paterson had changed his face. He was totally naked—and circumcised.

"Hey," Joey said, staring at the sketch, "I look . . . uh, I mean, *that* guy looks good."

"So, is it obscene?" Paterson said.

I hesitated. I wanted to make sure I gave the right answer. It was so weird, I wasn't really sure what the whole thing meant. "Well . . . "

Paterson interrupted. "First, you should know that it's 'T-a-l-e-s,' and not 'T-a-i-l-s' of Missing Pieces,' which apparently someone in the administration thought it was. And, second, you should know that it has to do with what we all talked about that day at the Steak 'n Shake when Miss Alicia told Kayla she needed surgery."

Joey and I looked at each other. All I could remember from that day was feeling really uncomfortable talking about my breasts in front of Gray. And it was happening again.

"You remember," Gray said, "about the fairy tales."

"Oh, yeah," I said, "something about *Cinderella* and *The Little Mermaid,* right?" I looked at the pictures. "I get it. In this picture the girl has no toes, and in this one the girl has no tongue, like the fairy tales. And then this one is like the story *The Red Shoes.*" I avoided the picture of the girl without breasts. I knew that one was no fairy tale and I wasn't going to bring the whole thing up again.

Joey pointed to the middle picture. "But *this guy* still has a dick," he said, then added in a whisper, "Thank God."

"Yes," Paterson said, "*This guy* still has a penis because men aren't raised on tales about giving up body parts to achieve their dreams, even though, according to Freud, it's supposedly their biggest fear."

"The old castration complex," Joey said.

Gray nodded in agreement.

"So what are you going to do about your project?" I asked. "Can you do another one?"

Paterson walked to where Gray was sitting next to a horse sculpture. "You mean something acceptable and noncontroversial like this horse here." Then she walked toward a painting of a rain forest. "Or maybe these trees. Look at this, how could anyone paint a picture of a rain forest without irony, without the political implications? Art is supposed to make you think."

Gray moved away from the horse. "I totally agree. Why does anything that challenges the status quo have to be seen as threatening?"

Paterson continued her rant. "What am I supposed to do? Put the women's body parts back in and remove the penis? Then what will it say? Instead of 'Tales of Missing Pieces,' maybe I could call it 'Tales of a Dickless Administration.' At least it would be saying something about censorship."

I knew from past experiences with Paterson's outrage that I wasn't required to say anything at this point.

"Can you imagine?" she continued. "Kovac says, and I quote, 'The school district's policies allow for the removal of anything that causes embarrassment or disrupts the educational process.' " She turned toward me. "Does this cause you embarrassment?"

I shook my head vigorously.

Then she glared at Joey. "Does this disrupt your educational process?"

Joey looked a little nervous, like he hadn't really been paying attention. "No?"

Gray walked over and studied the sketches. "Have you thought about protesting?"

"I thought that's what she was doing now," Joey said.

Gray smiled. "I mean getting a group together to let everyone know that the administration is trying to censor you. Maybe even getting some of the teachers involved."

"Do you think anyone would go up against Kovac?" I said. "What about Etch A Sketch, what did he think?"

Paterson picked up the cloth and threw it over her arm. "At first, he didn't get it. But when I explained it to him, he thought it was really good. He even helped me with the title."

"So then what happened?" I said.

"He backed down as soon as Kovac came in to approve the preliminary sketches. Suddenly it wasn't acceptable."

"No balls," Gray said.

Joey snickered. "Hey, he could be in the picture. Now that would make a statement. Etch A Sketch with no balls."

Paterson even had to laugh at that one, but only for a second. "The final project is due in five weeks. I don't have any ideas as good as this one. I've got to figure out a way to use this."

Her lament was interrupted by the final bell. Gray

picked up his backpack. "I've got to go, but if you need any support, I'm here. I'll help you organize a protest if you want."

Paterson put the cloth back over the canvas. "Thanks, I'll think about it. How about you guys? Think you could get the dance department behind a rally?"

"I don't know," I said. "Our art doesn't really make you think. It's just sort of, you know, pretty."

Joey began dancing around the room, singing "I feel pretty. Oh so pretty . . . "

Gray, who shook his head and laughed, was already used to Joey's clowning around and seemed to think he was as funny as Paterson and I did. Yup. Gray Foster was definitely looking like boyfriend material. He turned to me. "I'll pick you up around seven tomorrow night?"

Since school had been all about red shoes and rehearsals during the week, I hadn't really had a chance to get excited about the date. "Sure," I said, feeling that familiar flutter in my stomach. "Seven's good."

He turned to Paterson. "You've got to fight this," he said. "That's what creativity is all about." He shook his head. "This *is* supposed to be an art school."

Chapter 9

By the time Gray arrived on Saturday night, my parents and Paterson had already left the house for the evening. A lucky break for me. No awkward introductions. No talk about portraits and penises. Just Gray and me on our way to his mother's poetry reading.

The university was nearby, so there was no time for embarrassing silences in the car. Plus, there was always enough going on at Farts to talk about.

Once we were in the auditorium, the lights dimmed immediately and the program started. I'd never been to a poetry reading before, and I was feeling pretty proud of myself for being able to understand the first poet. But when Gray's mother came out to read her work, it wasn't as easy to follow. I caught a reference to Icarus—I'd learned about him when we'd studied mythology—but I couldn't connect the image to the rest of the poem. Then there was one about a set of dishes that I couldn't grasp at all. When the reading was over, so many students and teachers went up to the stage that Gray gave his mom a wave and told me we didn't have to wait. Whew. I wasn't sure if they gave quizzes after those kinds of things.

As he steered out of the parking lot and pulled into the nearest gas station, Gray turned to me. "My mom said I could use her car if I promised to get it washed. I didn't have time to do it before the poetry reading. I hope you don't mind? It will only take a couple of minutes."

"No," I said, "it's fine." I figured it might give me enough time to make up something semi-intelligent to say about his mother's poems.

He fed a five-dollar bill into the machine. The green light flashed, "FORWARD, FORWARD," then suddenly turned red and flashed, "SLOWLY, SLOWLY, SLOWLY," then "STOP." The car jolted.

I was about to tell Gray that I'd really enjoyed the readings when I suddenly felt a strange sensation—as if we were going forward, but I knew we weren't.

"Are you okay?" Gray asked.

"It seemed like we were moving."

Gray smiled. "Yeah, when the machine starts to come toward you, that happens."

I looked up. The windshield went white, covered in soapy crystals. Then a giant brush headed toward us. I ducked involuntarily.

Gray smiled again. "You don't go through car washes much, huh?"

I laughed self-consciously. "When I was three my mother took me through, and I screamed the whole time. After that, she left me home. Now I know why. It's a little bit scary—if you're three, I mean."

Gray's blue eyes sparkled. The side brushes gently rocked the car. "Paterson and I wash her car by hand," I added. I wasn't sure if I was babbling but I was suddenly even more nervous when I realized how close we were sitting in the darkened car.

"So what did you think of the poetry reading?"

"It was great," I said. "Your mom was good and so was that other poet, the one who read the Barbie poems. I liked how she made fun of all the dolls like Ken and Midge."

"She teaches with my mom," Gray said.

"I thought she should have had one called Bulimic Barbie, but I guess it's hard to find something that rhymes with vomit."

Gray thought for a minute. "There's comet," he said, laughing. "Anyway, she's published a whole book of those poems. We'll have to look for it."

The sign in front of us started blinking, "HOT WAX, HOT WAX." My stomach was doing *changements*. He said *we*. He thinks we're a *we*!

As streams of liquid zigzagged down the windshield in random patterns, I tried to think of something to say about his mother's poems, but the truth was that I didn't really understand any of them. "Your mother's poems were good," I said, hoping I didn't sound like too much of a liar.

Gray laughed. "It's okay. I don't understand most of them either. I keep telling her she's got to write for real people because not everyone understands all the allusions she's making. But I see where she's coming from. Sort of like Paterson."

"What do you mean?"

Gray raised his voice over the whooshing sound of the hot-air vents. "You've got to do your own art, make your own statement, not let anyone else tell you what to do."

I stared at the droplets on the windshield. They looked like tiny ballerinas dashing from side to side in formations, blind to the force compelling them to run. Then suddenly some of them dispersed and began dancing upward, defying gravity. The light turned green and we drove forward.

"That was fun," I said.

"I promise our next date will be more conventional."

Our next date. I liked the sound of the words in my head.

Gray looked at his watch. "Want to go to the Oasis? It's still early."

The Oasis was the place everyone from Farts went to on weekend nights. There was a huge movie theater, a zillion restaurants, and a great ice-cream place. The only problem was the security guards, who made everyone keep moving all the time. It was like if two people stopped to talk, a riot was going to break out. My mom had said it was for our safety too, but sometimes it didn't feel like it. So when we ran into Paterson and some of her friends from the art department, we immediately moved into the ice-cream place and sat down before the guard could tell us to "walk along."

I wasn't all that thrilled about my date turning into a group meeting, but I had to admit the nervousness factor definitely went down a notch with my sister and her friends there. After Paterson introduced us to the people we didn't know, someone brought up the subject of her art project.

"Have you thought about that protest?" Gray asked.

Paterson's friends perked up when they heard the word. A guy named Ryan, with platinum hair spiked about six inches high, announced, "We think it's a great idea. I could get my dad to cover it."

I knew Ryan's dad was a reporter for Channel Seven, but I didn't think Paterson's art project would be *that* newsworthy.

Sara, a friend of Paterson's who shared her affinity for iridescent hair coloring, chimed in. "I saw a kid on TV who dyed his hair green and got suspended and this organization called the AC-something got him back in school somehow."

"It's the ACLU, the American Civil Liberties Union," Gray said. "My dad's a lawyer. He did some work for them back in New York."

"But I'm not suspended." Paterson licked whipped cream off her lips. "What are they going to do for me?"

Ryan twirled his silver skull earring. "Maybe they could force the school to accept your project."

"Maybe," Sara said. "The kid on TV still had green hair." She ran her fingers through her own lilac locks. "They decided it was his constitutional right to have whatever hair color he wanted."

The rest of the conversation centered on planning the protest and listing names of people they thought would get involved. I had a weird feeling about the whole thing, like maybe they didn't know what they were getting into, but I kept quiet. I had my own issues to deal with: red shoes, breast reductions, not to mention my date with Gray and how it was going to end.

Turned out the date thing wasn't worth worrying about. By the time the ice-cream was eaten and the protest was planned, it was so late I offered to get a ride home with Paterson. Gray's mom had mentioned his curfew, and I'd already figured out if he took me home he wouldn't make it. He tried to tell me he didn't care, but I knew he did. He might have been an advocate for free speech, but I could tell he wouldn't want to get in trouble with his mother. Besides, he was the first guy I'd ever dated who looked at my eyes the whole night. I wanted to make sure he was allowed to go on a second date with me.

I was a little disappointed with the friendly hug at the end of the evening. I'd been hoping for something more. But I was willing to wait.

Joey had been busy the whole weekend again so when we met after school on Monday, Paterson and I had to fill him in on the protest thing.

We were standing in front of the cafeteria, taking a

break before rehearsal. "I'm not sure I want to be a part of this," Joey said.

Paterson sipped a raspberry ice tea. "You're already a part of it—a *big* part of it."

"Thanks," Joey said with a grin, "but I'm not sure I want my big part displayed in front of the whole school."

"Don't be crazy," Paterson said. "I changed your face. No one knows it's you. Ryan and Sara didn't even recognize any of the people in the sketches."

That was a relief. Even though I was fully clothed in the picture, I didn't want any more people focusing on my anatomy. I hadn't told anyone yet, but I'd seriously been considering seeing the doctor Miss Alicia had recommended—just to see what he'd say. I didn't need a resurgence of the Knock off the Knockers vs. Keep the Cantaloupes campaign.

I looked at my watch. "We'd better get to rehearsal," I said. "We don't want to keep Timm or any of his *em*s waiting." I was finding it hard to get over my bitterness toward him.

Joey laughed. "He's not such a bad guy."

"Sure," I said, as we approached the backstage area. "You've got a principal role in his ballet. Try hanging out with Devin and Karen—with Officer Ballanchine breathing down your neck."

"Devin alone would be enough for me to lose it,"

Joey said. He dropped his dance bag behind the curtain and raced to the stage.

It turned out Timm wouldn't be rehearsing my part right away, so I found a place in the audience and took out my calculus book.

After a few minutes, I heard a familiar voice from behind me. "Hey, I thought I'd find you here."

Gray dropped a book into my lap. The cover featured a zaftig Barbie eating what looked like a piece of strawberry shortcake. I laughed. "Where'd you get this?"

"My mom had a copy. She said you could borrow it," Gray said. "I checked, though. No 'Bulimic Barbie.' Maybe you should write your own poem."

"I don't think I'm much of a poet," I said. "I'm more spatial than verbal, and I've got the test scores to prove it."

Gray pulled the seat cushion down and sat next to me. "There's a lot of poetry in dance," he said. "Maybe you could do *Bulimic Barbie: The Ballet.*"

I laughed. "Maybe." I studied the cover of the book. Even though Barbie's breasts, hips, and thighs were huge, her waist was tiny. "This reminds me of something I saw on TV."

"It does?"

"Something about evolution. Researchers found that the best measurements for childbearing had to do with dividing your hip size into your waist measurement and getting zero point seven or something like that. They said all the great sex symbols like Marilyn Monroe were zero point seven and that's why men loved them, because the male brain was hardwired to want women who would be good reproducers."

"But Marilyn Monroe didn't have any children."

"Yeah," I said. "Go figure. Anyway, Paterson said it was a load of crap and just another way for men to explain why they're attracted to empty-headed women with tiny waists. She said she'd bet that all the researchers were men."

"Or women with zero point seven whatever," Gray said. "Men aren't the only villains."

"I should know," I said, laughing. "I'm an ugly step-sister. I'm oppressing Cinderella."

"And you're being oppressed too," Gray said.

"You mean by the prince?"

"No," Gray said. "In real life—by getting that part."

"Oh, yeah," I said. "My good friend, Timm."

"You know you have alternatives," Gray said.

I didn't answer him. I wasn't sure if he was referring to the surgery. It was bad enough that day at Steak 'n' Shake when Paterson brought it up. Now it was just the two of us.

"There are other . . . you know, types of . . . dance companies," Gray said.

I let out the breath I was subconsciously holding.

"It's pretty obvious your talents are being wasted as a stepsister."

I looked down at my pointe shoes. "Yeah, well, maybe next time."

"I'm serious," he said. "You know, there have been a lot of dancers who didn't have the right . . . umm . . . look for ballet. I mean, look at Judith Jamison."

I'd seen Judith Jamison dance in a special on TV before she was head of the Alvin Ailey company. It was true; she didn't look like a typical dancer. For one thing, she was African American, and for another she was extremely tall. She was a beautiful dancer, though. One of the best. "But she was Judith Jamison," I said.

"Well, you're Kayla Callaway."

"Which means?"

"You're good. There are plenty of dance companies that would be happy to have you and that don't require stick-figure dancers. I've seen some of them perform in New York."

"I don't know," I said.

"Judith Jamison found a place for herself," he said, "and so could you."

I folded my arms in front of me. "Maybe."

"You could even be a choreographer and run your own company of unconventional-looking dancers. Then you wouldn't be oppressing anyone."

"What's this about someone being obsessed?"

Gray and I looked a few rows behind us. Officer B. was sitting by himself in an end seat. I wondered how long he'd been there and how much he'd heard.

I tried not to laugh. "Umm . . . we said *oppressed*."

"Oh, well, that's okay then," he said, with his low, scary cop voice. He stood, glared at Gray, then walked toward the stage.

Gray's eyes opened wide. "What was that all about?"

"He thinks Devin or Karen or I might have something to do with the red shoes thing."

"What?" Gray said. "That *you* might have put them up?"

I shook my head. "No, that we might be targets because we're wearing red shoes in the ballet."

Gray's face turned serious. "You don't think you're in any danger, do you?"

"I don't know. I thought it was just someone making trouble, but now I'm starting to wonder."

Gray leaned toward me. "But you're not scared, are you? I mean, it's not affecting your dancing or anything, is it?"

I shrugged. "I don't think so."

Gray started to say something, but then Timm called the step trio to the stage. I got up and adjusted my leotard. "Thanks for the book," I said.

"No problem. Keep it as long as you want. But remember—*Bulimic Barbie*." He swept his hand in the air as if the words were already on a marquee. "*The Ballet*."

I pretended to put my finger down my throat and *bourréed* toward the stage steps.

That night I decided to bring up the subject of plastic surgery with my mother. Paterson had already gone to bed, and my mom and I were alone in the kitchen when my dad walked in. I thought he might leave when he figured out what we were talking about. He usually let my mom do the "girl talk." But, surprisingly, he stayed.

"I've had several patients who've had plastic surgery," he said, pulling out a kitchen chair.

I wasn't crazy about being compared to someone that my father counseled on a weekly basis, but I figured I'd listen.

"I think you have to ask yourself some questions before making a decision like that," he said. His voice suddenly went from parent tone to professional speak.

"What questions?" I said.

"What do you expect to gain from this surgery?"

"Smaller breasts?"

He laughed. "Yes, but how do you think this will

change your life? Are your expectations reasonable?"

My mother set out three cups of mint tea. I lifted the cup, but the steam was too hot on my nose. "I don't understand what you mean."

My father grasped his mug. "What do you think will happen if you have this surgery? Instant self-confidence? Instant ballerina stardom?"

"I'm not that stupid," I snapped.

The steam from my father's cup rose like fog. "I know that. But these are the questions you have to ask yourself."

I thought about it. I was a good dancer. Maybe even a great dancer compared to some of the others at Farts. But . . . I hesitated before trying to explain. "Becoming a ballerina involves a combination of talent, looks, hard work, and luck. The only one of those things that most dancers have any real control over is the hard work. But in my case it's different."

My mother sat in the chair next to me. "What do you mean?"

"Usually in ballet if you have a problem like bad turnout or short muscular legs with a too long torso, you can't change that. But I can change my body to fit the ballerina mold. It's an opportunity to give myself another advantage."

My parents nodded.

"I don't think this surgery will guarantee my success," I said. "But at least I'd have a shot at it. Without the surgery, I don't. No way."

My father took a sip of tea and nodded. "I see you've thought about this a lot."

I shrugged, warming my hands on the mug. I guessed it had been on my mind, subconsciously. More than I'd thought. Suddenly I was saying things that I'd never really put into words. My father, the psychologist, really *did* know what he was doing.

"There's one more thing you should think about," he said. "What about your self-image?"

My tea was finally cool enough to drink. I felt the warmth in my throat as I stared at him questioningly.

"I think you have to examine exactly how much of your identity is tied up in having large . . . umm . . ."

My mother finished his sentence. "Breasts."

I sat back in my chair abruptly. "I'm not some slut who flashes them around in tight shirts if that's what you mean."

My mother patted my hand. "Your father knows that, sweetie. But he's just trying to point out how different you'll look."

My father nodded. "Yes, yes. I just mean . . . how do you see yourself? Do you see your . . . umm . . . *breasts* as an integral part of your identity?"

I hadn't really thought about that. It was too bad I couldn't go around without them for a day or so. Someone who wanted implants could just stuff her bra with balloons to see how it would feel, how people would react. But there was no way I could take mine away temporarily. For me, the decision would be permanent.

Before I could admit I wasn't sure about that one, my mother intervened. "I think what you really need to do is talk to a professional about this."

"I thought dad was a professional," I said.

My mother laughed. "I mean a plastic surgeon."

My father got up from his chair. "Your mother's right. It's always good to get several opinions."

My dad was always looking for several opinions. That was one of the things I liked about him. Once he and my mom had decided Paterson and I were going to go the arts route, he researched the best places for us to take lessons. He'd even looked at the last five years of standardized test scores at Farts before giving in to Patersons's begging.

"We'll make some calls tomorrow," my mother said. "Ask around about who has a good reputation."

I pulled out the rumpled business card that I'd stuck in my pocket before starting the whole conversation.

My father bent over to look at it. "Andersen Marlowe.

He has an excellent reputation. Several of my patients have gone to him."

Now this was the stuff Dad was good for—knowing about doctors, not ballet and boobs. I mean, he and my mom both appreciated my dancing and Paterson's art too, but I knew neither of them could identify with loving something so much that you didn't mind doing it twenty hours a day if you had to. They liked their professions well enough, but teaching and psychology just weren't the same as dancing and drawing.

My mother picked up the card and stuck it by the phone. "We'll call tomorrow, then." She smiled at me. "Okay?"

I shrugged. "Sure, sounds good." I looked at my father. "Thanks," I said. And I meant it. But I really hoped that would be the last time I had to engage in conversation with my father about my intimate body parts.

Chapter 10

Somehow my mother had managed to get an appointment for that Friday. I was glad I didn't have to think about it for too long, but mad that I was missing seeing Gray. He and Paterson were meeting to talk about the next day's protest strategy session. I definitely would have preferred being with Gray talking boycotts than being with a plastic surgeon talking boobs.

The waiting room didn't have that funny smell you usually associate with doctors's offices. It smelled normal, whatever that is. I was really starting to hate that word *normal*. I'd never realized how much people threw it around all the time. The reason I was sitting in this doctor's office was because my breasts apparently weren't "normal." Until Miss Alicia had given me Dr. Marlowe's card, I hadn't really seen myself as abnormal.

I looked down at the paperwork my mother was filling out—things like insurance company numbers and whether I'd ever had gall bladder surgery. There was a list of about fifty things that could be checked off: allergies, asthma, bleeding, colitis. . . . It was a virtual alphabet of afflictions. I didn't know so many things could go wrong with one body. I was pretty much only worried about two things—and both were double D.

Mom and I had told Paterson we had to drive to a special store to find a bra to wear with my costume. I wanted to make my own judgments about the surgery and Dr. Marlowe, without Paterson bombarding me with her theories. I understood her position, but I wanted to get another opinion—even if it meant being on the same side of the argument as such vastly different factions as Timm with two *em*s and a group of flat-chested high school girls who seemed to see me as some sort of rival in a bizarre mammary match. And, as much as I hated to admit it, Miss Alicia was right. There might not be a place for me in the traditional world of ballet. I loved dancing, loved the feel of a perfect *pirouette* or an effortless *grande jeté*. Why else had I spent all these years in a dance studio, with sore muscles and bloody toes, if I wasn't going to be a ballerina? But did I have to be a "traditional" ballerina? Was there a place for me—and my boobs—somewhere else in the dance world?

I looked around the room and tried to take my mind off the fact that in a little while I was going to be talking to a perfect stranger about my breasts. An older couple sat on the pink and purple flowered couch next to ours. I was trying to figure out why they were there when the nurse called both of them in, leaving my mother and me alone in the waiting room.

"What do you think they're having done?" I said.

My mother shrugged. "I don't know—maybe their kids got them joint face-lifts for a fiftieth anniversary present. Maybe a two-for-one deal."

I wasn't sure if she was serious. Sometimes after teaching third grade all day, the sarcasm she'd been holding in for hours just spurted out. "Would *you* want a gift like that someday?"

"Not unless I'm really hideous. Was it you or Paterson who had chicken pox?"

I could see my mother was preoccupied with the paperwork, so I searched for something else to distract me. As I reached for a magazine, I noticed a small poster on the table that read WHO SAYS ONLY FAMOUS PEOPLE HAVE PLASTIC SURGERY? Under a picture of an attractive blond woman it read CERTAINLY NOT SUSAN. SHE'S ONE OF OVER A

MILLION AMERICANS WHO CHOOSE TO IMPROVE THEIR LOOKS—AND HOW THEY LOOK AT THEMSELVES—THROUGH PLASTIC SURGERY EACH YEAR. SHE CALLED THE AMERICAN SOCIETY OF PLASTIC SURGEONS TO FIND A PLASTIC SURGEON. I guessed she wasn't as fortunate as I was to have someone shove a doctor's card in her hand after suggesting a rack reduction.

As I surveyed the room, I found several similar posters. There was: WHO SAYS ONLY PEOPLE OVER FORTY HAVE PLASTIC SURGERY? CERTAINLY NOT CHRISTINE. And then there was: WHO SAYS ONLY WOMEN HAVE PLASTIC SURGERY? CERTAINLY NOT JIM. Jim was wearing white boxers and a white bathrobe, opened in front. He looked like a soap opera star. I wondered if the picture had been taken before or after the surgery. Upon further reading, I learned that Jim was ONE OF 70,000 MEN IN THE UNITED STATES WHO CHOOSE TO IMPROVE THEIR LOOKS EVERY YEAR.

I did the math—a total of one million Americans who'd had plastic surgery minus 70,000 men. That meant that every year more than 930,000 women thought they needed to enhance their appearances. I pictured the student body at Farts. There was no way that many of the guys were better looking than the girls.

After I finished learning about Susan, Christine, and Jim, I searched the coffee table for a magazine. There were all sorts of choices—*Seventeen, Soap Opera Digest, GQ.* I wondered if at the last minute, patients picked out a face or body they wanted and brought the magazine in with them. I pictured the doctor looking down at the magazine and then up at the patient and shaking his head sadly.

I didn't feel like looking at computer-enhanced pictures of beautiful people, so I picked up a Sesame Street book instead to try to remember what it was like before I became "abnormal." I turned to the first page. At the bottom, under the picture, someone had written, WHO SAYS PLASTIC SURGERY IS ONLY FOR REAL PEOPLE? CERTAINLY NOT BERT AND ERNIE.

I chuckled, thinking I'd like to be friends with the person who wrote that. I was about to show my mother the book when she got up to give the nurse the first page of the paperwork. The nurse thanked her and gestured toward the door to the examining rooms. "You can go right in now."

I turned back to my new friends Susan, Christine, and Jim. I wondered which of their body parts had tingled as they walked through the plastic surgeon's office for the first time.

As I hoisted myself up onto the vinyl examining table, the wide white paper rustled beneath me. I was glad the nurse hadn't handed me one of those skimpy paper gowns—I could never get them to stay closed in front. I looked down at my feet, dangling from the table. It reminded me of the times my mother would let me sit on the kitchen counter while she was cooking. Had I known I'd eventually be dangling my legs from a plastic surgeon's table and contemplating breast reduction surgery, I definitely would have appreciated how simple my life was then.

My mother, who was finally done filling out more forms about my most intimate bodily functions, put the clipboard down and sat in the chair next to me. "Are you nervous?"

"A little."

"Don't worry," she said. "You don't have to make any decisions today. It's just a consultation."

I rested my hands on the table behind me. The crunch of the paper was deafening in the quiet room. Packages of gauze, sponges, rubber gloves, and humongous Q-tips stood neatly against the back of the desk. I imagined the doctor standing on a stool, cleaning the ears of a gigantic patient, though that probably wasn't what the Q-tips were for. Above the desk, next to the medical degrees and diplomas, there was a poster of a cartoon. It pictured a truck with the word LIPOSUCTION written on the outside. A huge snake-like hose extended from the back of the bulging truck and through the front door of a place called Fairtree Medical Center. Ahh, I thought, a little plastic surgeon humor. Was that a good thing? Did I really want a funny plastic surgeon?

"You know whatever you choose to do will be fine with your father and me," my mother added. "This is your decision."

I wondered how such an important thing could suddenly be my decision. After so many years of "Look both ways before you cross the street" and "Make sure you call me before you leave the party," how could something as important as altering my body parts suddenly be just "my decision"? It didn't seem right. For my whole life, my parents had told me the same things over and over, making sure I did exactly what they wanted me to do, and then when I really needed them to make an important decision for me, they were like, "Sorry, we're outta here."

I was just about to say something to make my mother feel guilty about all that when the door opened.

Dr. Marlowe didn't look the way I'd expected him to look, which was sort of like Jim, from the picture in the waiting room. I figured if he had access to free plastic surgery, why not look like a soap star? But Dr. Marlowe looked, well . . . normal. Medium height and build. Short hair. No beard or mustache. No visible signs of abnormality. But then again, he probably got a discount for fixing those things.

After the introductions, the first question Dr.

Marlowe asked me was, "What are your goals?"

I hesitated. "To be a principal dancer in a ballet company."

Dr. Marlowe smiled. "I meant surgically, but you've answered my next question, why you want smaller breasts."

My dangling feet swung involuntarily. I wasn't sure if I was supposed to answer.

Dr. Marlowe continued asking questions, sometimes duplicating the extensive biography my mother had just written. "What about family history?"

I looked at my mother.

Dr. Marlowe turned toward her too. "Are there any other members of your family with large breasts?" I had never met anyone, man or woman, who could say the word *breasts* so many times with such a serious face.

"My great-grandmother was rumored to be large," my mother said, adding, "I guess it skipped a couple of generations."

She made it sound as if it were some kind of genetic defect, like being color-blind or having eleven toes. If Dr. Marlowe hadn't had such an easy manner about him, I might have felt like a freak.

He asked me a lot more questions, and then said he was obliged for legal and medical reasons to tell me all the things that could go wrong. I braced myself.

"There's a low incidence of complications," he said, but then quickly added something about anaphylactic shock. I wasn't sure what that was, but it didn't sound good. The look on my face must have concerned him, because he quickly assured me that in nineteen years, he'd never seen it happen. He went on about the slight chance of losing nipple feeling as well as the ability to breast-feed. By now my feet were swinging beneath me like crazy.

During our whole conversation, Dr. Marlowe was writing furiously in a folder, but at a certain point he came toward me with his pen. I thought for a second that he was going to write on me, but he moved toward the paper sheet I was sitting on instead. "This is the type of scar you will most likely have," he said. He drew a straight line and what looked like a large smile underneath it. "It's called an anchor scar—because it looks like a boat anchor." He then drew another type of scar, one with a straight line and a circle on top. "This one's a lollipop scar," he explained. "But because of your size, you'll most likely have an anchor scar. The trade-off is size for scars, and the benefits are proportion and function. It will be easier to exercise, and you'll get rid of the rashes underneath your breasts."

I wondered how he knew about the rashes. Then I

realized how many breasts he must have seen. In fact, a lot of the guys at Farts probably thought Dr. Marlowe's profession was some kind of dream job.

"Now what size were you thinking of?" Dr. Marlowe said.

I looked at my mother. She stared at me with a blank look. I had never really thought I'd have an opportunity to choose my size. "Umm, maybe B, or A, or somewhere in-between."

The doctor wrote in a folder.

"Wait a minute," I said. "If I go between sizes, will I be able to find a bra to fit me?"

"Certainly," he said. "It'll be much easier than it is now."

That was good news. Every time I finally found one that fit, the company would stop making it. And the salespeople weren't any help either. Once when I'd asked a department store clerk if she had a bra that would make me look two sizes smaller, she'd answered, "Honey, I sell brassieres, not delusions." Then she showed me something called The Minimizer. It sounded like a movie with a heroically challenged action star. I ended up buying two of them, but it didn't make any difference. My breasts still hurt when my feet left the ground.

Dr. Marlowe continued talking about what the surgery would entail: about five hours in the operating room, ten days of recovery, two weeks of sponge baths, yuck.

"I have to warn you," Dr. Marlowe said. "Sometimes when girls in their teens have this surgery, there's a chance they aren't finished growing. But I think it's probable that you won't get any bigger."

I hadn't even thought of that possibility.

"It's good that you're thinking of this now," he continued, "when it's just your decision."

"What do you mean?" I said. "Who else's decision would it be?"

Dr. Marlowe looked up from his folder. "I've had cases where a husband doesn't want his wife to have the surgery for some reason or other."

I could imagine what Paterson would say about that.

"Usually I tell the patient to split five pounds of apples into two bags and connect them with a rope, then have the husband wear it around his neck with the apples in front. After a few hours, the husband gets the idea."

My mother laughed knowingly.

Dr. Marlowe skipped the physical examination, saying that if I decided to have the surgery, he'd take measurements at the next appointment.

That was a relief.

He started to explain some things about insurance

to my mother, but I had already stopped listening. I couldn't help thinking of that phrase "Damned if you do; damned if you don't." I finally understood what it meant. If I went ahead with the surgery, I would be giving in to the demands of the whole ballet world that refused to let me and other women be individuals, to look the way we did and still perform. But if I didn't have the surgery, I would be giving in to all those jerks at school who didn't care about me at all, but just wanted to ogle. And I'd never be able to dance in a ballet company. Either way, I was letting someone else dictate the design of my body, the same way fashion designers somehow get women to fit their squared-off toes into pointy shoes.

When my mother and I finally left Dr. Marlowe's office, there were a few more people in the waiting room with various bandages. It occurred to me then that beauty was a lot like ballet. The bar had been raised there, too. It wasn't because of talent and tenacity, though. It was because of technology.

It made me think of an old *Twilight Zone* episode my parents made Paterson and me watch on the Sci-Fi channel one night. They said it was a classic. It opened with a group of doctors and nurses taking the bandages off a woman's face. She was hoping the operation worked and that she'd look pretty like everyone else. When the last bandage was finally rolled off, you saw her face and it was beautiful. Then you heard everyone gasp. "It didn't work," they said disgustedly as the cameras turned on the doctors and nurses. All of them had pig faces.

Chapter 11

Gray said his mother didn't mind if we used their house to plan the protest. He'd been raised on rallies and demonstrations. Even though his parents had been divorced for a long time, one thing they agreed on was free expression. He said he'd been making posters for picket lines since he was old enough to use a Magic Marker.

In the two weeks since Gray had suggested a protest, Paterson and her friends had gathered a large and diverse group together. Most of the theater department had gotten involved, taking time away from rehearsing their latest production, *Crucible, The Musical!* Gray said they saw the whole Paterson thing as a "witch hunt" and decided to get involved. I didn't want to rain on his crusade, but I knew a lot of those drama kids and for some of them, it was just another chance for them to be . . . well, dramatic.

Paterson, Joey, and I got to Gray's house before anyone else. I'd been dying to see him. Ever since our first date, we'd tried to get together again. But between ballet and my doctor's appointment, things hadn't worked out. He'd come to a few rehearsals, but we were never alone. We had big plans for the next time we were both free. Gray said he knew about a really cool place where they did improvisational comedy. And there was this great sushi bar he wanted to take me to. But when was all this going to happen? The more our dates were delayed, the more I couldn't stop thinking about him. My mind was turning to mush.

When I found out that once again we were going to be surrounded by other people, I tried to put my hormones on hold. Gray had said something about going out after the meeting, but we hadn't planned anything definite. I was really anxious to find out where this thing was headed. Was I just someone to hang out with while he was at Farts? Or was there more going on here?

Gray let us in and gave me a lingering hug. It would have to be enough for now, I thought. The house seemed sort of weird, not what I'd pictured. There were gold brocade couches with animal claw feet, lace doilies on dark wood tables with lots of knickknacks and vases and old photographs all over the walls. I stopped in front of a picture of an old man in a safari suit, carrying a rifle and standing next to the carcass of an animal I didn't recognize. "Is this your grandfather?"

Gray looked at the photograph and began laughing hysterically.

Paterson and Joey came over to see what was so funny. I looked at them, baffled. I hadn't thought it was that stupid a question. "I'm sorry," Gray said, "but if you knew my grandfather, you'd understand why I'm laughing. He hates hunting and he hates guns, not to mention the fact that he wouldn't be caught dead in a safari suit. He's the most left-wing, liberal person I know."

"So who's this guy?" Joey said.

Gray picked up the picture and stared at it. "I have no idea. It came with the house." He put down the frame and swept his hand through the air like Vanna White. "With all the rest of this stuff."

I scanned the room again. "Huh?"

"We had to rent the house furnished. It belongs to some old couple who decided to go on a world tour. Our apartment in New York is the exact opposite of this. My mom's books take up most of the living room, and we only have one black leather couch and two chairs. No vases. No little, breakable people."

"Whew," Joey said. "I was beginning to think I was totally wrong about you."

"What do you mean?" Gray said.

Joey picked up a container sprouting a colorful fake bouquet. "You know the whole rebel without a vase thing. I thought you were more Guns N' Roses rather than—"

"Rifles and artificial flowers?" Gray said, finishing Joey's sentence. He laughed. "Don't worry, you know the real me."

We were interrupted by the entrance of a large group of potential protestors carrying poster boards. There were a lot of kids I'd never even seen before. I wasn't sure if the whole picket thing was a good idea, but Gray and Paterson were really into it. Joey didn't seem to be that interested in free speech, but I think he felt guilty that he hadn't been hanging around with us much lately.

While Gray directed Paterson and the rest of the gang to the garage, where they were going to set up work stations, I stayed in the living room, looking at all the pictures. I thought it must be weird to live in a house surrounded by strangers looking at you all the time.

"I see you're getting to know the family," said a voice from behind me.

I turned to find Gray's mother with an armload of

books and her glasses down low on her nose. "Umm, I thought you weren't related to these people," I said.

Gray's mother laughed. "I'm kidding."

I wanted to address her directly, but I'd forgotten the last name she used. It wasn't Foster, like Gray's. Instead, I just asked how her work was going.

"Good," she said. "But time has just flown by. I was hoping to have finished writing my paper on Atwood, in between teaching and lecturing. Now the semester's almost over."

"Atwood?"

"Yes, Margaret Atwood—have you read her work?"

"No, but I think they read something by her in AP English senior year."

"She's a wonderful poet and novelist. I've been writing about the use of fairy tales and myth in her poetry—"

Gray snuck up from behind me. "Don't bother with the poetry. Read *The Handmaid's Tale*—it's her best work."

"Oh, we could argue this forever," Gray's mother said. "I'll leave you two alone. I've got work to do. Nice seeing you, Kayla." She disappeared into a hallway.

I looked at Gray with a puzzled expression.

"It's a running joke we have. *The Handmaid's Tale* is one of my favorite books. It's sort of dark and futuristic. But my mother's always trying to get me to read

Atwood's poetry. Every once in a while, she'll type up one of the poems and leave it on my desk."

I couldn't help but think about how Gray and his mother led such different lives than most people I knew. It was amazing to me that they actually talked to each other about novels and poetry. My parents read books when we were on vacation, but most of the time my dad read journals about psychology and my mom read third-grade books, stories about kids swallowing turtles and stuff like that. Once in a while they'd mention some interesting thing they'd read somewhere or another, but there were no great debates going on, no running literature jokes.

Gray came closer to me. "So, how are you doing?"

I smiled. "Pretty good."

"We getting together later?"

My heart started beating faster. This was definitely not the way someone who just wanted to be friends would have asked that question. "Sure," I said.

He took my hands in his and drew me closer. I was positive he could hear the pounding in my chest. The backs of my thighs were starting to tingle.

As he dropped my hands and slid his arms around my back, Paterson yelled from the doorway of the garage. "Hey, you guys, can we get a little help here? We need markers and things—the whole crew's here now."

I desperately wanted to ignore Paterson and wait to see where the moment was going, but I also didn't want her barging in on us. I pulled away from Gray and whispered, "I guess we'd better go."

Gray smiled. "You want to help me get the markers? They're in my room."

I followed Gray down a dark hallway. I had never been in a guy's bedroom before—at least, not a guy that I liked. Joey didn't really count. Part of me wanted to race into the room, slam the door, and smash up against Gray. The other part, the realistic part, knew that wasn't going to happen with his mom in a room close by and a bunch of protest-planning dissidents in the garage.

Gray's bedroom wasn't furnished as unusually as the living room—no pictures of dead animals or anything. There was one odd thing, though. In each of the three corners of the room sat a guitar, painted periwinkle blue.

I pointed to one of them. "What's this?"

Gray picked one up and began strumming lightly. "It was my sophomore year art project at my high school in Manhattan. I called it 'Blue Guitar.'"

For a second I thought he was kidding. It didn't look like any art project I'd ever seen—not even some of Paterson's strange sculptures made from McDonald's containers and bubblegum. I tried to look as if I understood what he was talking about, but I was pretty sure I wasn't hiding my confusion very well.

Gray laughed. "Don't worry," he said, "you kind of had to be there. It was a weird school. Kids did all kinds of bizarre projects. Paterson's paintings would have been hailed as creative or innovative instead of subversive."

"I guess that's the difference between New York and here," I said.

"Among others," he added, staring right into my eyes. "Some of them not so bad."

He laid the guitar on the bed and took my hand. As he drew me closer and put his arm around my waist, I could feel his breath on my face. He smelled lemony. I lifted my chin and looked into his eyes as he swept the hair off my shoulder. His fingers brushed my neck, causing a small lightning bolt to rush through me. I'd been waiting for this since our first date.

I put my arms around his waist as his lips moved toward mine. Then Paterson yelled from down the hall, "About those markers, guys . . ."

We broke apart and stared for a second into each other's eyes. "Oops," I said. "I forgot we were on a mission."

Gray gave a huge sigh and mumbled, "Yeah."

I thought my blood would never stop racing as we grabbed the tubs of markers and walked back down the hall, shoulder to shoulder. I felt as if I was floating across a stage in a spectacular *pas de deux*. But the minute I spotted Paterson, my thoughts turned to the revenge I was going to exact on her for having the absolute worst timing of anyone in the entire world.

I recognized Ryan and Sara and a few other people who were laying out posters and stencils of block letters in the garage. We were ready to form an assembly line until everyone realized we had forgotten the most important thing—a slogan that would express Paterson's outrage.

"What exactly are we trying to convey?" Ryan asked. His hair was spiked unusually high.

Paterson took a marker out of her mouth. "I guess it should have something to do with censorship. . . ."

"And the idea of having to cover up the beauty of a naked body," Sara added.

Everyone was quiet for a minute or two, thinking. Then Joey broke in with, "Hey, how about 'No Nudes is Bad Nudes'?"

Paterson groaned. "Please, can we keep the bad puns to a minimum?"

Gray picked up a red Magic Marker and rolled it between his palms. "What about the idea of patriarchy's need to conceal the penis?"

Joey looked up from his poster. "Gray," he said, "you're a fine man, but I think I speak for most of us here when I say, 'What the hell are you talking about?'"

Everyone laughed. But I liked the fact that Gray was an intellectual type, that he wasn't afraid to say words like *patriarchy* and risk being labeled as weird. Paterson was the only one I'd ever heard mention patriarchy. And that was after she had taken a women's studies course in New York.

"Wait a minute," Paterson said. "Gray's right. You rarely see a penis exposed in art. Women's bodies are all over the place. Especially breasts. The only time you find penises are in work by homosexuals, like Mapplethorpe."

"So, what's wrong with that?" Joey said.

Paterson waved her paintbrush like a sword. "Nothing, but you don't see Brad Pitt or George Clooney letting it all hang out on the silver screen—"

Gray interrupted her. "But nudity for actresses is considered practically mandatory."

"That's right," Paterson said. "Even Oscar winners like Gwyneth Paltrow have to flash a little boob to get noticed."

Joey seemed to be in his own world. "I've got it," he said, raising a ruler. "'Free Willy.'"

"Willy?" I said.

Joey puffed up his chest. "Not everyone has a Saint Rocco, you know. Some guys just have a willy."

While everyone else burst into fits of laughter, Ryan

seemed particularly uncomfortable with the way the conversation was going. He squirmed on the floor next to his poster. Another drama guy sitting on an old crate tried to cross his legs and almost fell. It was fun to see the conversation focused on men's anatomy for a change—instead of mine. And it was really interesting to see how self-conscious the guys became.

"Hey, I've got another one," Joey yelled. "How about 'Stop Hiding the Salami'?"

"That could have a whole other meaning," someone said.

"We need to somehow refer to freedom of speech," Paterson said. She thought for a minute. "How about 'Bare,'—as in *b-a-r-e*—'Witness to the First Amendment.'"

"I don't know," I said. "I don't think anyone in administration or on the school board would get it. They'd probably use it as an excuse to show how high-school kids can't spell these days."

Gray, who had been quiet for a while, suddenly began poking out letters from the large black stencil pages. We all watched curiously. When he was through punching, he laid the words out on a poster: "The Penis Mightier Than Censorship."

After a few seconds of thoughtful silence, Paterson shouted, "It's perfect. It's got it all—the body, the power of art, and the First Amendment. What else could we want?"

We all agreed with her—except Joey. "Wait a minute, I've got one more you'll love. How about, 'What's Wrong with Schlong?'"

Paterson laughed and threw her paintbrush at him. "Enough," she said. "Let's get to work."

After a short discussion of logistics, we decided it would be best to outline the phrase on one of the posters and cut out the letters to make a giant stencil. Then we'd use markers and paints to fill in the letters. As we took turns using the stencil, some of the drama kids sang songs from the musical. It was the first time I'd worked with other people for a common cause like this, and it felt really good. Gray's mom ordered pizza and we ate in the garage, surrounded by posters, swapping stories about teachers. Just as I was beginning to relax and forget about all the troubles of the past few weeks, Sara brought up the red shoes. "I heard someone's stalking some of the dancers," she said to Joey and me.

Gray glanced at me, then stood and asked if anyone wanted another drink.

"It's nothing. We don't really know what it's all about." I wasn't in the mood to give the whole history of the dance department, particularly my relationship with Melissa. I still thought she had something to do with it.

I just hadn't figured out what. "I'll go help with the sodas," I said.

In the kitchen Gray popped open a can of Sprite and handed it to me. White foam bubbled at the teardrop opening and then turned transparent, spreading across the metal lid. As I took a sip, invisible bubbles tickled my nose. "So, what do you think?" Gray said.

"About what?"

"The whole protest thing."

I nodded a few times. "Interesting."

Gray laughed. "You're not really into it, huh?"

That wasn't exactly true. It was just that I'd never been the protesting type. When you're a ballet dancer, you kind of do what everyone tells you to do. Point your foot this way. Move your arm that way. You just don't ever think of rebelling. If someone told you that you needed to lose a few pounds, you went on a diet. If someone told you to get breast reduction surgery, you considered it. "I'm not really used to protesting," I said. "A ballet studio is one of the few places where if someone tells you to jump, you're literally supposed to ask how high."

Gray laughed. "I never thought about it that way." He handed me a couple cans of soda to take back to the garage. When we got there, Joey was holding a poster over his head and dancing between the markers and old milk crates. The theater group was belting out the play's finale, "Burned in the U.S.A." Even Paterson and her friends had worked up a rap number, though they seemed to be having trouble rhyming with the word *censorship*.

Gray looked at me. "So now what do you think of civil disobedience?"

"Looks like fun," I said just as Joey grabbed my arm in an attempt to turn his *pas de deux* with the sign into a *pas de trois*. I tried to hang onto the sodas, but I ended up spilling my Sprite all over myself. Just what I needed—a wet T-shirt contest right there in Gray's garage. I pulled away from Joey and yanked the bottom of my shirt about a foot in front of me. I looked at Gray. "Umm, do you by any chance have something else I could wear?"

"Sure," he said, "follow me." I was a little more nervous going to his bedroom again, remembering what had *almost* happened the last time we were in there. But when we got there, Gray just told me to take any shirt I wanted out of his closet and then closed the door behind him. I took my time looking at his shirts, not so much to find one to wear, but to find out more about Gray.

I looked for the biggest shirt I could find—a plain black T—and then threw my wet one on the floor. I slipped the shirt on and checked myself out in the long mirror attached to the back of the door.

I tucked it into my jeans and then bloused it out a little. Satisfied that it looked okay, I bent to get my own T-shirt off the floor. Just as I grabbed the sleeve, I spotted a strip of red fabric. I started to pick it up, thinking it might be one of those ribbons kids get during Drug Awareness Week. But as I tugged on it, something from under the bed trailed behind. I could practically hear my hammering heartbeat as I saw the familiar shape.

A red pointe shoe.

My hands shook as I reached for its mate and pulled it out. I examined both slippers. The paint was dry and cracking in some places, just like the ones I'd handled the first day they appeared in school. I looked at the bottoms of the shoes to see if they could provide a clue as to who had originally owned them, but nothing showed through the paint. I stared at the slippers. What did this mean? And why did Gray have them?

I'd hung onto the idea that Melissa was behind the whole thing for so long because I didn't want to believe that I was really in danger. For a while I'd even thought the shoes might have been meant for Devin. But now I couldn't hide it from myself any longer. The message was definitely meant for me. And not only that, it was from someone I had trusted and liked, maybe liked a little too much. My whole body was trembling. How was this possible? In the span of an hour, Gray Foster had gone from crush to criminal.

I wasn't sure how long I'd been frozen in that spot, but suddenly I heard a knock and Gray's voice asking me if I found something. "If not," he called through the door, "I could look in my mom's closet."

"N—n—no, it's okay," I said. "I'll be out in a minute." I shoved the pointe shoes back under the bed and picked up my T-shirt.

By the time I returned to the garage, everything was almost cleaned up. The posters were drying and everyone was trying to coordinate the rally. Their voices became a blur of sounds, like background music in a scary movie: *I Know What You Have Hiding Under Your Bed.*

I watched Gray's lips move as he began to explain that he would transport the signs to school on Monday morning and everyone could meet at six in the parking lot to coordinate. It was like watching a pop-up video on VH1. In my mind I saw signs bursting up around him that told a different story from what he was actually saying. One card read, "I'm the one who put up the red shoes." Another one read, "I'm stalking Kayla Callaway."

The back of my neck began to throb. I raced over to Paterson and whispered, "Can we please leave—now?"

At first she cocked her head and just stared at me. But I must have looked like I meant it, because she grabbed Joey and wrapped up the conversation quickly. I slipped out of the garage and into the backseat of Paterson's car, and in a couple seconds Joey and Paterson hopped in and we pulled out of the driveway. I felt as if I'd just gotten off the Tower of Terror ride at MGM.

Paterson turned off of Gray's block. "What's wrong?" she said. "Was it the T-shirt thing?"

Joey turned around. "Sorry," he said. "I didn't mean it."

I shook my head. "You are not going to believe what I found out—"

"Oh my God," Joey blurted. "I meant to tell you."

I stared at him. "You knew?"

"Umm, yeah, for a couple of days."

"Why didn't you tell me?"

Joey shrugged. "I thought you'd be upset."

"*Upset*?" I screamed. "*Upset* isn't the word."

Paterson banged on the steering wheel. "*Hello!* Could someone tell me what's going on here?"

I got as far as "When I was in Gray's bedroom . . ." when I heard what Joey was saying at the same time. I wasn't sure if I'd heard right. "What?" I said.

"I got into Ballet on the Beach," he repeated.

Once I processed the information, I screamed, "Oh my God! That's fantastic!"

Joey glared at me. "Are you bipolar or something?

Weren't you just going nuts on me about it?"

"I thought you were talking about something else." I could hold onto my news for a few minutes. Joey's story was a lot better than mine was. "Tell us how. Tell us everything."

He turned his body around to face Paterson. "You know how I've been busy a lot on weekends and stuff? Well, Timm's been working with me on some of my technique so I could audition for the company. And . . . that's where I was last week. A couple of days ago at rehearsal, Timm told me I got in. I start touring with them right after graduation."

I threw my arms around Joey's neck, as far as the seat-belt would let me. "That's unbelievable! I'm so happy for you."

Joey gave a tentative smile. "But you hate Timm."

"I don't hate *you*," I said. "Ballet on the Beach is a great company."

"You mean you don't mind that I'll be working with Timm?"

Paterson slapped Joey on the thigh. "What kind of person do you think she is? We're both happy for you. If I weren't driving, I'd hug you too."

Joey smiled. "So you'll come watch the perfor-mances? You won't boycott?"

"You idiot," I said. "Just don't expect me to applaud

when they call Timm out on stage."

"As long as you give me a standing O, that's all I care about. Hey, what were you going to say before?"

I thought about those stupid shoes under Gray's bed. Did I want to bring the whole thing up while we were so happy for Joey? I decided it could wait. First I wanted to figure out exactly what I was going to do about that two-faced jerk.

Chapter 12

The first time the phone rang the next day I looked at the caller ID and decided not to answer it. After a minute or two, I dialed voice mail and listened to the message: "Hey Kayla, it's Gray. You left in a hurry yesterday. I thought we were getting together this weekend. Give me a call. Maybe we can go to a movie or something."

Fat chance.

Just as I slammed the receiver down, Paterson passed by the door of my room. She rubbed her wet, newly pink hair with a towel. "Who was that?"

"Gray."

"How come it rang so many times?"

"Couldn't get to it."

Paterson threw the towel on my bed and plopped down. "What did he want?"

"I don't know . . . to go out or something," I said, picking up the towel and folding it.

"So are you going to call him back and tell him yes?"

I shook the towel out and proceeded to match the corners again. "No, I don't really feel like it. I've got stuff to do."

Paterson bounced on the bed. "Stuff? You've been wanting to go out with this guy since you met him and now that he asks you on a second date, you've got stuff?"

I avoided looking her in the eye. "Yeah," I said. "You know, calculus homework, that kind of stuff."

"Okay, now I know something is wrong." Paterson put my pillow up against the headboard and leaned against it with her arms folded. "The day you want to do math homework instead of go out with Gray Foster—"

I interrupted her. "I just don't feel well, okay?"

She sat up in a lotus position. "Is it the Joey thing?"

For a second I wasn't sure what the Joey thing was. Then I got a vision of Timm's bald spot in the mirror. "No, I'm happy for Joey. I really am." It sounded sincere. I wondered if I really meant it. Since I'd seen the shoes under Gray's bed, I hadn't thought too much about Joey going to Ballet on the Beach. Joining a company right from high school wasn't something I ever considered. All I'd wanted was a decent part in the school production of *Cinderella*. I'd always planned on going to college to study ballet for a few years. I really was happy for Joey.

I turned on the TV and sat at the other end of the bed. An *I Love Lucy* marathon had started with my favorite episode—the one where Lucy and Ethel get a job in a candy factory and the chocolates start coming down the conveyor belt so fast that they can't keep up with them. Lucy was stuffing a handful down her shirt when the phone rang. I looked at the caller ID. "Don't answer it," I snapped.

Paterson gave me a strange look, then glanced at the tiny screen on the phone. "'G. Foster'? Don't you at least want to tell him you don't feel well?"

"No."

"What if he doesn't want to talk to you at all? What if he wants to talk to me about the protest? Can't I answer it?"

I hadn't thought of that. He'd called back so soon. I saw it more as stalking behavior than maybe wanting to talk to Paterson.

Turned out Paterson's question was rhetorical anyway. She lifted the receiver before it went to voice mail. My head pounded as I listened to her talk to Gray about the plans for the next morning. I waved my arms at her and mouthed, "Tell him I'm not home."

"Sure," she said. "We'll all meet in the parking lot across the street. Umm . . ."

I held my breath and waved my arms some more.

"No. I'll have her call you when she gets in. See you in the morning." She turned to me as she hung up. "Okay, what's going on? What happened yesterday? Did he pull something when you guys were in his room or something?"

I scowled at her. "No," I said. I couldn't even imagine that. Gray wasn't that kind of guy. Then again, I hadn't pegged him for someone who made death threats either.

Paterson sat in the chair next to the phone and swiveled from side to side. "Then what is it? You know you can't hide anything from me."

She was right. I'd never kept a secret from her for more than about twenty-four hours. It was only a matter of time. "Remember yesterday in the car when I started to tell you guys what I found out?"

"Yeah, but you said it was no big deal."

"Well, it was. It was a huge deal. After my shirt got wet, and I went into Gray's room to find another one to—"

Paterson slapped the arm of the chair. "I knew it. Guys are such pigs. What did he do?"

"Will you give it up? He didn't do anything. Although you're probably right about most guys being pigs." I flexed my feet, then turned my toes under again. "I almost wish he were just a pig. When I went to pick up my shirt that fell on the floor, I saw something sticking out from under his bed. I pulled it out to see what it was and—"

"Porn," Paterson yelled out as if she'd discovered penicillin.

"Are you going to let me tell this story? Porn would have been an improvement, believe me."

Paterson scrunched her eyebrows together.

"It was a pair of red pointe shoes," I blurted.

"What?" She hit both arms of the chair this time.

"Red pointe shoes. Spray painted. Just like the ones in school. And unless he's going to surprise us by standing in for Devin as the stepmother, I don't think they were his."

Paterson leaned forward and put her elbows on her knees. "What do you think he's doing with them?"

"Obviously, he's the one who put the first four pairs up. He was probably going to put up more, but when the school increased security, he apparently chickened out."

"But why?" Paterson said. "What possible reason could he have for doing it?"

"Oh, I don't know. Maybe because he's a *psycho*?"

Paterson leaned back. "Have you been getting any stalker vibes from him?"

I thought for a minute. We'd only been on one date, and that was in a really public place. On the phone earlier, he'd suggested a movie. Did stalkers take their stalkees to movies? "I don't know. He did come to rehearsal a few times."

"Have you ever seen him lurking?"

I curled my toes under until my instep stung. "Lurking?"

"Yeah, you know, like behind the curtain when you're dancing or around the dressing room after you're done."

I thought for a minute. "It's hard to distinguish between waiting and lurking. Sometimes he waits for me after dance class, and we walk to meet you and Joey."

Paterson grabbed a bottle of gel from the nightstand and squirted a sticky, translucent gob into her palm. "Sounds more like a lover than a lurker."

"Then how do you explain the shoes and the death threats?"

"Let's think," Paterson said as she spiked her hair up like a troll doll. "Maybe the shoes aren't meant for you. Maybe they're for someone else."

"Who? Karen? Gray didn't even meet her until a week ago. Devin?"

Paterson jumped off the bed. "That's it. Devin. He knows Devin's always been after you and he's jealous. Or he's defending your honor. Or something like that."

I was flattered for a minute. No one had ever defended my honor before. "But that's sick," I said, suddenly realizing what Paterson was saying. "You mean he'd threaten Devin just so he could impress me?"

Paterson shrugged. "Maybe."

I tried to think about it objectively. It was possible that I could have sparked some sort of psychotic possessiveness that would result in a jealous rage. But it didn't seem very probable. I'd never even dated anyone more than a couple of times. I started to think more clearly. "Even if Gray had somehow figured out that Devin and Karen and I were wearing red shoes, the motives just aren't there."

Paterson was quiet for a minute. She flipped a page of the Degas calendar hanging beside my bed. "You're right. We hadn't even known Gray that well when the first shoes appeared. Wasn't it right after that time we all went to Steak 'n Shake together? Gray couldn't have gotten enough information or worked up that much emotion in one afternoon to target anyone—not even you, my little siren of a sister. There's got to be another explanation."

I thought a minute. "Remember Melissa's initials

were on the first pair. Maybe they're in it together."

Paterson shook her head. "Ivy's the only one vapid enough to team up with her. Gray may be demented, but he's not dumb."

I was getting a headache from thinking when the phone rang again. Paterson looked at the screen. "'G. Foster.' He's not giving up. Maybe he is stalking you after all."

"What should I do?"

"Just answer it. He's not going to stop. You may as well get it over with."

I grabbed the receiver. "Hey," I said, trying to conceal my nervousness with a casual tone.

"Hey, it's Gray. Did you get my message?"

"Yeah."

"You ran off so fast yesterday. Were you okay?"

"Yeah." If finding out your potential dream guy is a crazed lunatic is okay with you.

"Good. Then do you want to go to a movie this afternoon—you know, the date we keep putting on hold?"

"Hold on a sec." I put my hand over the mouthpiece and told Paterson what he wanted.

"Tell him you know about the shoes," Paterson whispered.

"What? Are you nuts?"

"No, tell him you know. See what he says. Better to tell him over the phone. Safer."

I swallowed hard and took my hand off the mouthpiece. "I have one question first."

"Sure, what is it?"

"What are you doing with . . . umm . . . red pointe shoes under your bed?"

Dead silence.

"I can explain," he said.

So he wasn't even going to deny it or make up some story like the dog dragged them in or they belonged to the old couple who owned the house. "Go ahead," I said. "Explain away."

"I can't really do it over the phone—it's too complicated. Can you meet me somewhere?"

I covered the mouthpiece again and whispered to Paterson. "He wants to meet me somewhere."

"Go," she whispered. "I'll take you. We'll get Joey on the way, and we'll back you up if he tries anything funny. Tell him you'll meet him at the Oasis—in front of the movie theater."

"Umm, okay," I said, repeating Paterson's words, just like a ventriloquist's dummy. I hoped that wasn't prophetic and that I wasn't walking right into something stupid. I mouthed the word, "When?" to Paterson. She held up a finger.

"One hour?" I mouthed.

She nodded.

"In an hour," I said. I hoped Paterson knew what she was doing.

"So let me get this straight," Joey said from the backseat of the car. "Gray's the red shoe psycho?"

"The one and only," I said.

"But where did he get all the shoes? And why were Melissa's initials on the first pair? Are they in it together?"

"We ruled that out," I said. "I don't think Gray likes her any more than we do."

Paterson gasped. "Maybe he stole them because he has a shoe fetish. I read about that in psych class. It's all tied up in some kind of arrested sexual development."

"That's just what I need to hear," I said. "I'm not sure which is worse. And you guys are leaving me with him?"

"Don't worry," Paterson said. "We'll be watching."

I wasn't sure how Paterson and Joey were going to blend into the crowd with her pink hair and his newly blond tips, but I said okay. I just wanted to get the whole thing over with. I had way too much to think about. "It's not enough that I'm already stressed over the ballet and the boob thing and now this demonstration. . . ."

Joey chuckled to himself. "Ballets and boycotts and boobs. Oh my!"

I turned around. "What?"

"Nothing," Joey said. "You just reminded me of *The Wizard of Oz*. You're like Dorothy with all this stuff going on."

"Yeah," I said. "All this trouble because of a pair of red shoes."

Paterson and Joey dropped me off at the entrance to the Oasis. "Stay in front of the theater for a while. I'll park, and then Joey and I can watch you from behind a pole or something."

"Great," I said. "How wide do you think these poles are?"

"We'll hold our stomachs in," Joey said. "We'll be cool. Don't worry. Or do you want us to come with you?"

"No," Paterson said. "That'll ruin it. He'll feel threatened, and he might not tell the truth."

Paterson was right, but it didn't make me feel any better as I got out of the car.

Once I was in front of the movie theater, I relaxed a little. There was no way he would try anything there. Too many people. Too much security. The same security I'd hated before.

Paterson and Joey were going to meet me in a half hour, so the whole plan seemed pretty safe. Still, part of me wondered why I was giving him a chance to explain at all. Hadn't he already proven to be a major jerk? When I saw a couple waiting in the ticket line with their hands all over each other, I knew why I'd agreed to meet him. Hormones.

My stomach did a *grande jeté*. Was I that pathetic? Could I overlook the fact that Gray Foster was a death-threatening serial stalker just because he was hot?

Before I had a chance to answer, he was walking toward me. He had his hands in his pockets and a back-pack slung over one shoulder. What did he have in there? Even if it was a weapon, he wouldn't be stupid enough to use it in a public place in broad daylight . . . would he?

"Hey," he said, glancing nervously at his shoes and then up. He knew enough to keep his distance, but didn't look like someone about to grovel. "Thanks for meeting me on time."

How polite. Was that some kind of stalker etiquette? What were you supposed to say when your pursuer thanked you for your punctuality? "You're welcome" seemed a little too victimish. I just grunted.

Gray gestured toward the ice-cream place. "Do you want to get a drink or something?"

"No." I looked around for Paterson and Joey and glimpsed a puff of pink hair. "Let's just walk around here."

Crowds chattered and clutched their shopping bags as they bustled by the two of us walking in silence. I felt as if we were in a commercial where everyone had used the same deodorant but us. Then Gray broke the stillness. "This whole thing got so out of hand."

I put my fingers in my jeans pocket and felt the coins Paterson had given me to call her cell phone if we got separated. "So you only meant to stalk me a little then?"

Gray turned to me. "I didn't mean to stalk you at all."

"So you did it by accident?"

"No. I mean it wasn't about stalking. It was about art. It was an art project."

"On what? The art of stalking?" I stopped for a second, then remembered my own rule that we would keep walking the whole time.

"I'm telling you," Gray said, with impatience. "It had nothing to do with stalking. I didn't even know you'd be wearing red shoes in the ballet."

I was incredulous. And, strangely, a little disappointed. "So you didn't care who you were after—just any old dancer in red shoes would do?"

"I wasn't after anyone," Gray shouted. He let out a loud breath and shook his head in frustration. "Remember those blue guitars you saw in my room?"

"Don't try to change the subject."

"I'm not. The blue guitars were an art project, too."

"You told me that, but I don't see any connection." I didn't want to tell him that I didn't see a connection between blue guitars and art, either. If he were deluding himself about being an artist, I didn't want to be the one to tell him otherwise.

"Remember, I told you at my old school I painted those guitars blue. Well, I put them in places all over the school."

"And that's art?"

"No. I attached a note to each of the guitars. Just like I did with the shoes."

"You mean like, 'Playing blue guitars will kill you'?"

"No, nothing like that. It was a line from a Wallace Stevens poem."

"Who?"

"Wallace Stevens. He was a great poet from the early nineteen hundreds."

He could have been a great serial killer for all I knew. "But what does this have to do with the red shoes?"

Gray stopped and swung his backpack around to the front and started to unzip it. I looked around for Paterson and Joey and caught a glimpse of her head again. Thank goodness for passionate pink hair dye.

"Wallace Stevens wrote a poem called 'The Man with the Blue Guitar.' About the power of art. The guitar's a symbol of the imagination."

"And . . ."

"I thought it was a cool way to demonstrate the importance of art, the power of the imagination. The note said, 'Play it on the blue guitar.' It was kind of like an invitation to art, an invitation to use your imagination."

I thought about it. His explanation did seem possible. "But what does, 'Dancing in red shoes will kill you' have to do with the imagination or art?"

Gray pulled a book out of the backpack. "It doesn't. It has a whole different message." He handed me the book. "Turn to page forty-seven."

I flipped through it and came to a poem called "A Red Shirt."

"Look at the last line on the page," Gray said.

My eyes scanned the poem until it got to the words *Dancing in red shoes will kill you.*

"See?" Gray said.

"See what?"

"The words are from a poem, just like with the blue guitar. I was trying to merge art and poetry to send a message."

I was beginning to sense his frustration. I thought maybe I'd cut him some slack and try to understand. "Okay, so who was the message for?"

Gray looked down. "It was sort of . . . for you. But, really, for everyone."

Now it was my turn to be frustrated. "I'm sorry. I don't get what you're talking about."

"You know how I told you my mom makes me read poems that she's researching? Well this one's by that writer, Margaret Atwood, the one we talked about. The poem's about how girls are taught through fables and myths that they should always be careful, how fairy tales tell them they shouldn't wear red and go in the woods. . . ."

"Like Little Red Riding Hood?"

"Yes, and they shouldn't dance in red shoes because they'll get their feet cut off."

"Paterson was right."

"What?"

"She said the shoes might have something to do with the fairy tale. . . . But what did it have to do with me?"

Gray put the book in his backpack. "After you found out why that Timm guy didn't choose you for a lead part and Paterson compared it to those fairy tales, I got to thinking about this poem my mom had given me. She said it meant that girls and women are taught to take the safe path all the time, to avoid risks. Dancing in red shoes is like not listening to all that and taking the risk."

"But why didn't you tell anyone that's what it all meant?"

Gray looked down and zipped his backpack. "I don't know. I chickened out. I assumed everyone would know it was art. Everyone at my old school in Manhattan would have."

"Really?"

"I think so. Anyway, when everyone started freaking out and talking about death threats, I got scared. I thought it would all just fade away if I stopped putting up the shoes."

I turned toward him. "So it didn't have anything to do with death threats at all?"

"No, I swear. I just wanted to do something different. To make people more aware of the sexist messages they get from everyday life. I was never going to hurt anyone." He looked me straight in the eye. "Least of all you."

I stared back at him. "Why least of all me?"

He stuffed his hands into his jean pockets. "Well, you must know that I really like you . . . a lot."

Those were the words I'd been wanting to hear. Yet I didn't know what to say. I just stared at him for a few seconds, but then I remembered something. "One more question," I demanded.

Gray looked sheepish. "What?"

"Why were Melissa's initials on the backs of the pointe shoes?"

Gray laughed.

"I don't see what's so funny."

"You would if you'd seen her in the school store, prancing around trying to get my attention. She came in to buy a new pair of shoes."

"That doesn't surprise me."

"When she was finally done trying a bunch of shoes on, she left her old ones on the floor. When I told her she'd forgotten them, she said I could have them as a souvenir to remember her by."

I could hear Melissa's voice, as sickening as six packs of NutraSweet. "And you took them?"

"What else could I do? I put them in a box behind the counter. I wasn't going to do anything with them. But then I got the idea for the project."

Gray finished his explanation just in time. Joey and Paterson apparently had decided the clock struck midnight. They popped out of nowhere beside us.

"So . . ." Paterson said, "what's up?"

In those brief moments before she and Joey materialized, I had almost forgotten the whole plan we'd devised. I gestured toward Paterson and Joey and looked at Gray. "You've met my bodyguards?"

After a brief summary of what had transpired, Paterson and Joey realized Gray was no longer a threat to me or anyone else. Paterson claimed she knew all the time it had something to do with the fairy tale and that Gray was a good guy. I didn't remind her about the psycho and smut suspicions, not to mention the fetish accusations.

"So what are you guys going to do now that you know?" Gray finally asked.

Joey shrugged. "Eat dinner?"

Paterson laughed. "Tell Etch A Sketch you deserve an A in class."

"I'm serious," Gray said. "You're all accessories now."

"Accessories to what—an art project?" Paterson said. "Since when is that a crime?"

Gray laughed. "Depends on the artist, I guess."

Paterson rolled her eyes. I knew she was thinking of some of her fellow art students. "I just have one more question," she said.

"What?"

"Did you really think anyone at Farts would get what you were trying to convey?"

Gray shrugged. "At my old school, we combined art forms all the time—poetry and sculpture, music and painting. It was kind of like a puzzle. Everyone liked trying to figure out what the artist meant."

Paterson shook her head. "You forgot we have a principal with the aesthetics of a slug and an art department head who thinks a single straight line is a thing of beauty."

Gray raised his right hand. "I promise I'll start sketching buildings or something."

"So let me get this straight," Joey said. "You're not a stalker? Never were a stalker?"

Gray laughed. "No."

Joey let out a sigh. "So now we can eat dinner, right?"

That night was the first in a long time I felt really relaxed. No one wanted to kill anyone. The red shoes mystery was solved. And, best of all, Gray Foster liked me—a lot. I played the day back in my mind. Dinner had been fun. We mostly talked about the protest plans. Before that, there was the whole explanation for Paterson and Joey. And before that, Gray had made his declaration of "like." That was the part I wanted to freeze-frame and play back my own way. If I'd been making the movie of my life, that's where Gray and I would have kissed. Before I fell asleep, I directed the scene, played the movie, and pressed the pause button just as our lips met.

Chapter 13

Normally getting up in the dark was not my idea of a good time, but on the day of the demonstration, brushing my teeth by morning moonlight didn't bother me a bit. It was going to be a great day. The protest was all about Paterson. No one at school was talking about my boobs anymore—they were all talking about a whole other part of the anatomy that I didn't have.

Paterson had told our parents what was happening, so at five-thirty they stumbled out of bed to wish us luck. They weren't quite as radical as Gray's parents, but they'd grown up in the sixties and got the whole fight-for-what-you-believe-in thing. "Just don't get kicked out of school," my mother yelled as Paterson grabbed two granola bars and ran out the door.

My father patted me on the shoulder. "Make sure things don't get out of hand."

"Sure, Dad." I smiled and followed Paterson to the car.

Paterson backed out of the driveway. "This is going to be so cool."

"Way cool," I answered, realizing we were probably talking about two different things. Now that I knew Gray wasn't a stalker, I couldn't stop fantasizing about being with him again. I felt a little guilty that my excitement about seeing Gray slightly overshadowed my enthusiasm for free speech. I tried to muster some outrage. "We're really going to kick butt."

When we got to the Burger King parking lot across the street from the school, Ryan, Sara, and Gray were already getting the posters out of the car. A few other cars pulled up and parked at the same time we did. As I grabbed one of the placards, Gray's arm brushed mine. Our eyes met and lingered for a second. My legs felt as if I'd just done a thousand *jetés*. We smiled briefly, but then it was back to business.

"Okay everyone," Gray announced, "here's the deal. The permit allows us to protest from six to eight A.M., as long as we're peaceful. The school can't do anything about that. But if we miss class, that's a problem."

Everyone groaned.

Gray closed the car door and gave me one last smile. "We've got to be in homeroom by the time the bell rings so Kovac doesn't have anything to complain about."

Ryan's blond spikes popped up next to Gray's dark ponytail. "My dad's sending the TV cameras around seven-fifteen so they can get the reaction from everyone arriving at school. We'll have to hurry and put the posters away around five to eight."

Gray nodded. "Okay. It's showtime."

The first hour of the protest was pretty uneventful. About twenty of us paced back and forth across the street from school, holding up our "The Pen-Is Mightier Than Censorship" posters. Some of the art majors who hadn't shown up at Gray's carried their own signs that read, "Farts Stinks of Censorship." Aside from the occasional junk-food junkies at the BK drive-thru, we were barely noticed. When we were, it was usually by someone yelling, "Hey, *penis* doesn't have a hyphen!" I was beginning to understand why so few people engaged in organized protest. No one seemed to care but the protesters.

Even Kovac had nothing to say as he drove past us and backed into his special space by the front entrance. Some of the art students crossing the street raised their fists in solidarity. Others who saw the signs but clearly had no idea what the protest was about, shouted "Penis Power" as they drove to their parking spaces and walked into school.

Around seven-thirty the theater majors put on a performance that they'd obviously planned ahead of time. Six of them piled their placards on the ground, lined up beside one another, and began to rap:

> We go to Farts
> and we're here to say
> we're trying to stop
> censorship today.
> Don't try to tell us
> that the penis is lewd
> 'Cause if you think it is
> check your pants—DUDE!

On the last word, in perfect sync, they all pulled their pant waists out and looked down at their crotches—even the girls.

It wasn't exactly Will Smith, or Will Shakespeare for that matter, but it got the point across. And it broke the boredom. It also prompted Joey to begin executing *grands jetés* and *pirouettes* up and down the street in front of the main entrance of the school. Not to be outdone, the theater kids repeated their rap, accompanied by an impromptu booty dance, behind Joey's leaps and turns. During the performance Gray and I took the opportunity to sneak back to the parking lot.

"Is everything okay with us now?" Gray said, leaning against his car.

"You mean since I found out the red shoes were all about a fairy tale instead of a felony?" I joked.

Gray laughed. "I guess that's what I mean." He reached for my hand. "Maybe we can finally have a real date soon."

I was about to say I'd like that too, but we were interrupted by the rest of the crew returning the posters. My frustration at never being alone with Gray was making me crazy. Classes were about to start, so we all grabbed our backpacks and headed off.

On the six o'clock news that night, Paterson's message was somewhat overshadowed by a sort of Lord of the Dance meets Sluts in the Street. So when a local radio station called the house that night wanting her to appear on the Hal Barker show the next night, she said, yes, without thinking about it. She was hoping to put some pressure on Kovac. Etch A Sketch, who had always liked Paterson and was secretly sympathetic to her cause, said the demonstration hadn't swayed the administration. Paterson thought maybe more publicity would help.

Our parents decided it would be a good idea for all of us to go to the show because the radio station shared a neighborhood with several gun shops and triple X bookstores, a connection I never understood. After a rousing session of raw porn, was it a guy's first impulse to go next door to buy a gun and fire off a few rounds?

When we arrived at the WADD offices, we were greeted by a guard and told to park in a fenced lot. Someone buzzed us into the building. I wondered if all the security was because the radio station feared crime in the neighborhood or because they feared the listeners. Hal, the DJ, was a Howard Stern wannabe who prided himself in antagonizing his South Florida audience of retirees, rednecks, and radicals. He was an equal-opportunity annoyance, never sticking to a particular point of view. He mainly wanted to stir up controversy, which is why Paterson agreed to go on the show. She figured he'd probably be on her side since that was the side getting the most flack.

After being buzzed in, we stood for a while in an empty hallway, wondering what to do. Finally a young woman who introduced herself as Sasha arrived. "You must be Paterson," she said, staring at Paterson's pink hair. "Too bad it's radio and not TV—that would look great on camera." She spoke in a breathy, husky voice.

Paterson put her hand up to her head. "Umm, thanks." She seemed a little nervous.

Sasha opened a door off the hallway. "You can wait in here until it's time to go on. I'll tell Hal you're here."

We stepped into a small room with two round tables and several chairs. Except for one man sitting alone at a table reading, the room was empty. It was deathly quiet, except for the low voices of the radio program being piped in.

I felt as if we were in a church or a library. "Do you still want to do this?" my father whispered to Paterson.

Paterson nodded.

The reading man looked up, and my mother took the opportunity to say hello. Ever the third-grade teacher, she was always trying to make sure no one felt left out. He nodded and returned to his book, but not before taking a good long look at my boobs.

Hal usually featured several guests with opposing viewpoints to stir up controversy. I was wondering whose side this guy was on when suddenly the door flew open. A man built like Humpty Dumpty shouted, "Are you ready to raise some Hal?"

I recognized the phrase from the few times I'd heard his show in the car, while surfing stations. My father extended his hand and began, "It's nice to meet . . ."

Hal ignored him and walked toward me. He looked

at my boobs, then at Paterson. "Who's she?" he said.

Paterson stood. "My sister."

"Does she go to the same school?"

"Yes," Paterson said.

"Then bring her on in. She can help us raise some Hal." His voice got louder on the "raise some Hal" part. I wondered if he ever got tired of saying that.

I looked at my parents to see how they felt about me joining Paterson. "Go on," my mother said. "It's fine." I think they felt better knowing Paterson would have some company. As I got up and followed Paterson to the door, Hal yelled out, "Hey, Reverend, let's go, the commercial break is almost over."

The other man closed his book, which turned out to be a Bible, and followed us out the door. We walked down another hallway, past some small rooms with large glass windows. I knew I wasn't one to talk, but as I watched Hal waddling in front of us, I couldn't help but think he really had a body made for radio.

When we entered one of the rooms, Hal sat at a control panel. Paterson and I sat near one microphone and the reverend sat at the other. He seemed to want to get as far away from us as possible, as if we had some catchy disease.

Hal put some headphones on top of his balding head and looked for a signal from Sasha, who was in a small booth next to us. She made one-two-three motions with her fingers and then one sweeping move, as if she were letting the trumpet section know it was its turn to play. But instead of music, we heard Hal in his booming voice utter his famous phrase yet again. "Are you ready to . . ." I noticed the reverend flinched every time he heard it.

Hal continued talking at lightning speed, characteristically raising his voice at the end of every phrase. "We're here with Paterson Callaway, a senior at Florida Arts High School who recently raised some Hal of her own when she unveiled her senior art project—a male nude surrounded by women." He accented the *round* in *surrounded*. "And we also have our favorite Bible-thumper, the Reverend Ronald Williams. So, Paterson, tell us about this project. I'm all for displaying the human body, I'm a regular at the nude beach myself, but *what* were you thinking?"

I tried to get the picture of Hal at a nude beach out of my mind as I listened to Paterson's response. "It isn't really about the nudity as much as it's about—"

Hal chimed. "What do you think of that, Reverend? It's not about the nudity."

The reverend grabbed the mike and brought it toward his mouth. "I've said it before and I'll say it again, we've got to bring prayer back into the schools. We've got to stop the drugs, the violence, and the fornication. We need—"

Hal broke in. "So what do you say to that, Paterson Callaway. Are you a fornicator?"

I wondered what happened to the questions about the First Amendment and censorship that Sasha had mentioned in the initial phone call. Paterson's mouth dropped open. She leaned toward the mike but couldn't speak at first. "N—n—no, my project has nothing to do with drugs or violence or . . . fornication. It has to do with how women are taught that—"

"Hey," Hal interrupted, "I'm noticing the reverend can't take his eyes off your sister's knockers." He looked at me. "What's your name, hon?"

"K—k—ayla," I whispered.

"I should say here that Kayla is Paterson's sister who is also a student at Florida Arts High and she's got some rack. What size are those things?"

I looked at Paterson, not sure how to answer. Before I could, she leaned toward the mike and said, "Getting back to my project . . ."

Hal broke in with, "And now I'd like to tell you a little about Dry Solutions Carpet Cleaning. . . ." He pressed a button and motioned to Sasha in the booth, then took his headphones off and turned toward us. "So what do you think? Wouldn't you like an exciting career in radio?"

Before we could answer, a tall man with shoulder-length hair stepped into the studio. Hal introduced him as Mark Somebody from the ACLU. I remembered Gray mentioned his father doing work for them. I heaved a sigh of relief that we'd have someone on our side.

Hal put his headphones back on and waited for Sasha's signal. "We're here with the Reverend Ronald Williams and high school student Paterson Callaway. They're duking it out over her controversial art project which prominently features the male organ. And I'm not talking about the one in the reverend's church, either. Joining us now is ACLU lawyer Mark Fuller. Mark, what do you think about penises displayed all over high school?"

Mark, who was sitting next to the reverend, leaned close to the mike so their faces were only inches from each other. "Hal, you know the ACLU's position on the First Amendment. We support the right to free speech, especially when it comes to art, even if it means a hundred penises."

Mark was no help at all. I could tell Paterson was getting frustrated. She grabbed the microphone in front of us and started talking really fast. "My project isn't about penises. It's about women and how they're taught that they've got to give up parts of themselves to be happy. My sister's a perfect example. She's a beautiful dancer, but if she wants to be a ballerina, she has to . . ."

I glared at Paterson. I couldn't believe she was bringing my boobs into the whole thing. Thankfully, Hal broke in once again. For a minute I thought it was a good thing that I wouldn't have to talk about my boobs in front of a radio audience, but then things took a turn, a double turn, for the worse. "A ballet student?" Hal continued. "So tell us about these killer rivalries in the school. I was going to save that for another show, but since you're here . . . I got an anonymous call just today concerning something about red shoes and death threats."

This time *my* mouth dropped open. Word had spread that Paterson was going on the show, but who would have called the station? Paterson grabbed the mike again. "That's all a misunderstanding. There were no death threats. It's an art project."

"Another art project?" Hal boomed. "Since when are death threats an art project?" He turned toward the reverend and Mark. "What do you guys think? Can the ACLU defend death threats as a work of art?"

Mark threw up his hands. "No comment."

"What do you think, Reverend? What's the church's position on the art of death threats?"

The reverend grabbed the microphone. "I've said it before and I'll say it again. If we could just bring Jesus back into people's lives . . ."

"This isn't about Jesus and it isn't about death threats," Paterson shouted into the mike. "The red shoes are a symbol. The phrase, 'Dancing in red shoes will kill you,' is a line from a poem. It's a metaphor. . . ."

"Whoa there, we don't use words like that on the radio," Hal shouted. "And tell me, how is it that you know so much about this? Could *you* be the one who put those red shoes all over the school?"

"N—n—no," Paterson answered.

"You seem to know an awful lot about them."

Paterson turned to me, her eyes fearful. If she told the truth, Gray would get in big trouble. I knew she didn't want to be a snitch. But she'd already showed that she knew way too much about the shoes.

Hal leaned forward. "Admit it," he shouted. "You're just a rabble-rouser. Art shmart. Paterson Callaway, you just want to make trouble, don't you?"

I moved closer to Paterson. "No she doesn't. She's an artist."

"Hey, it's the sister now—coming to the defense of her poor sociopath sibling," Hal shouted. He turned back to Paterson. "So how do you think this will look as a little footnote on your college application?"

I grabbed the mike without thinking. "It was me," I said. "I put up the red shoes."

I wasn't sure why I'd done it. I wanted to think it was out of some sense of social justice or selflessness. But, in reality, it probably had more to do with Gray. Even though it was his fault that we were suddenly in this mess, I definitely had a thing for him. And I didn't want him to hate Paterson and me for ratting him out.

Hal's eyebrows rose to where his hairline should have been. "Hey folks, how about that—the ballerina's a Hal raiser too. So, who'd you wanna off?"

I took a deep breath and sat straight in my chair. Suddenly I understood what the poem was all about. "The shoes are a message about how women are actually being taught to be scared. That it's our fault if we get kidnaped or drugged and then raped. It's like all those women-in-peril movies on the Lifetime channel. Even though the guy always gets it in the last few minutes of the movie, you've spent almost two hours terrified out of your mind. You can't undo that feeling with a quick bullet to the villain's head."

Paterson leaned forward. "It absolves men of their responsibilities and puts the blame on women for not being cautious. That's what the poem's about."

Hal looked over at the reverend and Mark again. "So what about it, you guys? You believe this poem crap?"

The reverend leaned forward. "The only poetry we need is the poetry of the prophets, telling us the stories of Jesus Christ, our Savior."

"Save it for Sunday, Reverend," Hal said. "How about you, Mark? What's the ACLU's position on poetry?"

"Hal, you know the ACLU supports the First Amendment right to free expression. That's why I'm here."

"But death threats, Mark? Surely the ACLU can't defend that."

Mark shook his head. "I'd have to know more about the case first."

"Folks, we're almost out of time. For those of you just tuning in, we've had the Callaway sisters here from Florida Arts High School. One's been raising Hal with penises at the school and the other, we just found out, is behind the red shoe death threats. Tune in to find out what happens to these sisters when the school gets a load of this." He turned toward the reverend and Mark. "Gentlemen, any last words?"

The reverend leaned forward. "Tonight in my prayers, I will ask God to forgive these girls and I will pray for their souls."

"There you have it, folks. Tune in tomorrow night when we're going to *raise some Hal* with animal rights activists. Now, a word about the Mattress Mart." He motioned toward Sasha and took off his headphones. "That was really something, girls." He leaned back and smiled as if we were all best friends.

Paterson and I were in shock. What had just gone on? Hal Barker didn't care about censorship. It was all an excuse to talk about sex and violence. Getting a confession out of me turned out to be an added bonus.

Paterson and I got up as Hal and the other men began shaking hands and joking with one another.

I followed Paterson toward the door. Stopped. And turned back. I faced the reverend and, at that moment, seriously compromised my position in the afterlife by shaking my boobs in his face. I pivoted and marched down the hall.

The car was silent for a minute. "So how did it go?" my father asked.

Paterson shifted in the backseat. "Couldn't you hear?"

"The volume was down so low, we couldn't make out what anyone was saying," my mother said, "except that phrase Hal yelled every few minutes."

"Yeah," I said. "It does get a little annoying." Paterson and I traded glances to determine exactly what we should reveal. I wondered how many of my parents' friends had been listening. I figured even if a few were fans of Hal's, they'd at least wait until morning to call.

I couldn't think about it. All I wanted to do was go home and go to bed. In the morning it might not seem so bad. Maybe by then Paterson and I would have figured out how to convince the school that the red shoes were all about social commentary and not social deviancy.

"So how did it go?" my mother said, echoing my father.

I turned to Paterson and put my index finger over my lips. She nodded. "Fine," she said, putting her head back on the seat. "But I think I'm through raising Hal for a while."

Chapter 14

I woke up the next morning with a feeling of total dread. How many people had listened to the radio show? Hal wasn't exactly Howard Stern, but he must have a decent-sized audience to stay on the air. I hoped it was some twisted part of the population that didn't have anything to do with my parents or school.

As soon as Paterson and I pulled into the parking lot, I realized that either Hal was more popular than I'd thought or Farts had a lot more deviants than I'd thought. The stares and whispers started immediately as Paterson and I made our way to homeroom.

For the third time in my life and in the same semester, I heard my name on the loudspeaker. "Would Kayla and Paterson Callaway please come to the principal's office, please." It was even before the pledge.

I dragged myself to Kovac's office, trying to contain my anger. Why hadn't Gray come forward in the beginning? And why did Paterson have to be so controversial all the time? Why couldn't she just be quiet and draw flowers or something? Even though they'd both taken the focus off me for a few weeks, things were worse than ever. Now I was a *psycho* with big boobs.

When I got to the main office, everyone stared at me in a new and different way while one of the secretaries led me to Kovac's private office. I was trying to figure out how I was going to get out of the whole thing without implicating Gray, when I inched through the door and . . . there he was, sitting next to Paterson.

Kovac gestured to a chair. "Have a seat, Miss Callaway."

I looked without expression at Paterson and Gray. I squeezed past Gray's knees, conscious that my butt was only inches from his face, and sat in the middle chair.

Kovac stared at me. "Mr. Foster tells me that this so-called project you spoke about on the radio was not yours, but rather *his* attempt at art. Is that true?"

I didn't know what to say. I'd watched enough cop shows to know about the whole technique of lying to one suspect about the other in order to coerce a confession. I thought for a minute. Usually they didn't do that with both suspects in the same room. I looked at Gray and then at Kovac.

"I already told you it's true," Gray said.

Kovac raised his eyebrows, expecting a response from me.

I nodded. "Yes, it's true."

"And how long have you known about this so-called art project?"

I cleared my throat. "Since . . . umm . . . Saturday."

"This past Saturday?"

I nodded.

"And it didn't occur to you to come forward with your knowledge, to come to me yesterday in school?"

"I . . . uh . . . we were busy with the protest and . . . uh . . . then I had rehearsal."

Kovac glared at Paterson. "Ah, yes, the protest. We'll get to that later." He turned back to me. "Miss Callaway, do you think the Hal Barker show was a proper forum for your . . . confession?"

"No, probably not."

"And yet you chose to air the school's dirty laundry on the airwaves with thousands of people listening."

Thousands? There went all hope of my parents not finding out. I swallowed hard. "I hadn't planned on even mentioning anything about the red shoes. It just came out because of Hal . . . you know, and the way he is."

Kovac nodded and turned to Gray. "Now, Mr. Foster, you say that this art project wasn't meant to be a threat to anyone." He said the words *art project* as if it was something you'd flush down a toilet.

Gray gestured to a book on Kovac's desk. "I told you if you would read the poem you'd understand."

Kovac looked down at the page for a few seconds. "Mr. Foster, I fail to see what this poem has to do with the threats you've made to the student body at Florida Arts High School." Apparently he'd taken a speed-reading course.

"Didn't you hear the explanation on the radio?" Paterson blurted.

Kovac glared at her. "I am not a fan of Mr. Hal Barker. I heard about your little dog and pony show from faculty members. They didn't go into detail." He turned toward Gray. "Mr. Foster, where did you get this book of poems, anyway?"

"My mother . . . she's a poet-in-residence at the university this semester."

Kovac made a face. "I don't know what you kids think you're trying to prove. I came to this school because I believed there were talented young artists here, artists who wanted to paint beautiful pictures. Instead I get death threats and penises." A spray of saliva punctuated his last sentence.

The three of us stared at him. It was obvious that further explanation would have been futile.

Kovac turned toward Paterson. "As for you and your *art project*, Miss Callaway. Don't think a little dancing in the street with posters over your heads is going to change school policy. That . . . *thing* will not be displayed at Florida Arts High."

After a tense pause, Paterson broke in. "Can we go back to class now?"

Kovac scowled at her. "Unfortunately, Miss Callaway, you may go back to class . . . unless, that is, you break any of the rules regarding my decision." He turned to Gray and me. "You two, however, may not return to class. I've called your parents, and they'll be here shortly."

My heart sank like a *grand plié* as Kovac walked to the door and looked into the main office.

"I'm sorry," Paterson mouthed to me.

I nodded. "It's okay," I mouthed back.

Paterson got up and attempted to inch through the opening of the door. Kovac opened it further, then closed the door behind them, leaving Gray and me in the office alone.

"How did he find out it was you?" I whispered.

Gray turned nervously toward the door. "He didn't. I came as soon as I heard your name. I wasn't going to let you take the rap. I heard what you said on the radio show. You didn't have to do that."

"I didn't want to get you in trouble. You confided in me. It wouldn't have been right."

"You didn't have to—"

I leaned over and kissed him quickly. "It's okay. I get what you were trying to do." I lowered my eyes, suddenly feeling shy about what I'd done. It wasn't quite how I'd envisioned our first kiss, but it would have to do. Then Gray leaned toward me and for a second I thought we might have an opportunity for another kiss, but the door burst open. Kovac burst through with my mother and Gray's mother trailing behind.

Once we were all seated, Kovac continued his spiel about beauty and art and death threats. He looked at Gray's mother first, then mine. Gray and I made faces at each other a few times when no one was looking. We had already heard it all and now it just sounded like blah, blah, blah, red shoes, blah blah, blah, Gray, blah, blah, blah, expulsion.

Yes. Expulsion. The administration apparently was not impressed with Gray's honesty or his creativity. "A death threat is a death threat," Kovac said. Not even Gray's mother's explanation of the poem could sway him. Gray was being kicked out of school because of the district's "zero-tolerance policy," a euphemism for "we have no idea where to draw the line and we're too lazy to figure it out, so we're just going to expel everyone who even talks about violence."

I, on the other hand, was merely suspended for a week. Because I had, in actuality, not made any threats myself, I was punished only for keeping the identity of the "perpetrator" a secret and not reporting him.

Neither Gray's mother nor mine looked very happy when we left the school in silence after gathering our belongings. I couldn't tell if it was Kovac or me my mother was mad at. I breathed a little easier in the car when she shook her head and said, "That principal is some piece of work."

That night we had a family meeting and decided that one sister on suspension was our quota. My parents said Paterson would have to find a way to express herself without a penis. Even though they understood that I had been trying to help a friend, they warned me that my suspension would not be a vacation. I was to keep up with my schoolwork and not leave the house or have visitors during the day. The only place I would be allowed to go would be rehearsals, because they were technically not part of the school day. Paterson would come home to get me and drive me back to school each day. I could take that.

Because we still had about six weeks left of school,

Gray's mother decided to send him to live with his father and finish the year at his old school. We said good-bye over the phone and he left two days later. *That* was a little tougher to take.

Were those red shoes worth all this?

Chapter 15

Paterson smiled and dropped a huge, thick envelope onto my bed. "From Gray," she said. He'd been gone two weeks and we'd been e-mailing almost every day, so the package was no surprise.

I threw down my European history book and tore the envelope open while Paterson plopped beside me. Several brochures, as well as a sealed card with my name on the envelope, fell out onto my rumpled sheets.

"What's this?" Paterson said, picking up the card.

I grabbed it from her and stuck it in my top drawer.

"Okay, okay, I get it," she said. "It's personal." She made a couple of smooching noises, picked up a pamphlet, and then read the words that Gray had highlighted: "dance major with concentration in choreography." She flipped it to the front. "And how about that? It's a college in New York." She grabbed another brochure. "New York," she said. Then another. "New York. Funny, there aren't any colleges in Kansas that specialize in dance."

I grabbed the brochure from her. "Very amusing," I said. "I don't remember you looking at art schools in Iowa."

"I chose New York because it has the best art school, not because it has the best boyfriend."

I threw the brochure at her. "I'm not looking at New York just because of Gray. They *do* have the best dance programs."

Paterson laughed. "I'm just messing with you. I think it'll be great if we're all together again in a year. I just wish it could be sooner."

I leaned my head back onto the pink satin shoe pillow at the foot of my bed. "Me too. I really miss Gray. I didn't think I would, considering I've only known him for seven weeks."

"But who's counting?" Paterson said with a laugh. "It does seem like he was around for a lot longer, doesn't it?" She unfolded one of the brochures. "So are you seriously considering choreography?"

I shrugged. "It never really crossed my mind until

you and Gray got me thinking with your art projects."

"What do you mean?"

"If I'm in charge, I can keep my boobs, shake up the dance world a little, and maybe help someone else who doesn't fit the ballet mold. Maybe someone who's overweight or in a wheelchair. Gray told me about a dancer he once saw in New York who performed with a prosthetic foot."

"Sounds like a plan," Paterson said. "Hey, c'mon in my room. I want to show you something."

I followed Paterson to the doorway. It was way too dangerous to step inside. She'd been trying to come up with something to replace "Tales of Missing Pieces," and the result looked like Hurricane Picasso had passed through. She waded through the junk to the big canvas that was housed in her room since Kovac had deemed it "obscene." "Look. I wasn't sure if it would work. But . . . what do you think?"

I stared blankly for a second. She had drawn a thick black line from one corner of the canvas to the other. The line passed right through the center of the picture and, consequently, right over Joey's penis. It looked like the "Just Say No" to drugs posters that were plastered all over school.

"You're not going to believe it, or maybe you will," Paterson said. "It was Etch A Sketch's idea. He said it was a way for me to keep the project *and* maintain its artistic integrity."

I nodded. "I get it. Something like, 'Just say no to women giving up their body parts, while men keep theirs.'"

"That's one way of looking at it," Paterson said. "It's also a commentary on the school's stupid rules about what's obscene. I'm calling it 'Tales of Censorship.' And there's no way the school can say it violates their policy now. "

"Kovac is going to be so pissed," I said with a grin.

Paterson rubbed her hands together like a witch over a bubbling cauldron. "I know. Isn't it great?"

Paterson moved some of the junk away from the canvas. "It's just too bad Gray won't see it. He'd get a kick out of it."

I stepped between two piles of squished paint tubes and stared wistfully at the picture of the foot with no toes. "He's not even going to see me be an ugly stepsister."

I left Paterson with her revenge, returned to my room, and ripped open Gray's card. The cover pictured a little girl in a tutu with her leg in a cast. Inside it read "Break a Leg." Even though he'd signed it just "Gray" and he was a week early, I thought it was the most romantic thing anyone had ever done.

On the morning of the ballet, I woke up with caterpillars in my stomach. Not butterflies. Butterflies were for big parts, not ugly stepsister parts.

During the week, we'd gone through the whole ballet several times. One time, I even got to be Cinderella. Just in case . . .

Just in case what?

Daydream Number One: *My life suddenly becomes a Broadway show. Lourdes twists her ankle or develops a pimple the size of a Volkswagen. She can't dance. I miraculously fit into her costumes. After the final* pas de deux, *I get a standing ovation and Timm with two* ems *says, "I knew you could do it," right before offering me a major spot in his dance company. I turn him down. Flat.*

Daydream Number Two: *My life suddenly becomes a Hollywood movie. Lourdes decides she wants to quit dancing because she meets a rich guy who opens up her eyes to the capitalism she never enjoyed in Cuba. She hands me the part at the last minute, and I'm brilliant. The whole thing ends with me surrounded by my fellow dancers, applauding my performance. And in the last shot I'm holding a bouquet of long-stemmed roses and getting a big, juicy kiss from Gray.*

When I saw Lourdes in her Cinderella costume that night, my daydreams faded like an old leotard. She looked beautiful, even in the tattered dress. As I watched her dance with the broom around the fireplace, I thought about what was coming next—the fairy godmother, the beautiful dress, the uncomfortable glass slippers, the prince. I suddenly realized I didn't want to be Cinderella after all. I didn't want to wear delicate slippers. I didn't want a guy who loved me because I fit a mold. No way.

I wanted to dance in scandalous slippers. Slippers that would have the whole world tsking under its breath.

I knew it for sure now. I wanted to dance in red shoes.

As I watched for my cue from Devin and Karen on the other side of the stage, Melissa snuck up behind me. "It's too bad Gray isn't here, huh?"

I didn't bother to answer.

"I guess if that person hadn't called Hal and mentioned the red shoes at school, the whole thing would have died down and he'd be sitting right there." She pointed to the audience.

I spun around and stared her right in the eye. "You called the radio station, didn't you?"

"I don't know what you're talking about," she said with a smirk.

"But how did you know it was Gray who put up the shoes?"

"I didn't. I always thought it had something to do

with you," she said. "I never guessed it was him. You just never know about some people."

"That's the difference between you and me," I said, preparing to leap onto the stage. "I've always known you were a bitch." I took one look back to see her tutu shimmy away with fury.

Fortunately, I was able to use my anger at Melissa to ham it up as the stepsister. With my adrenaline pumping, I felt like I was suspended in the air during my leaps. I whipped through the turns without a stumble. Even Devin looked impressed under his stepmother bonnet.

I admit that during the winter scene I was hoping Melissa would slip and fall. But the ballet went off without a hitch. Melissa and Ivy and all the other soloists were great. Joey and Lourdes were fabulous. And my little turn with the prince at the ball ended up getting spontaneous applause. Even though I wasn't supposed to outshine Cinderella, Joey made sure he held me tight enough to finish a quadruple *pirouette* and end in a perfect *penchée*, with my legs at a one-hundred-and-eighty-degree angle.

We all got three curtain calls at the end. And once we were offstage, Joey said he had to admit I was the best damn ugly stepsister Farts had ever seen. I gave him a huge hug and whispered, "You're a prince."

He drew back for a second. "Do you realize we may

never dance together again?" His face was serious.

My eyes welled up, and I couldn't answer. Nothing would ever be the same again after tonight. Not school. Not dancing. Not anything.

When Joey saw my reaction, he grabbed my hand and dragged me onto the stage. "One more *pas de deux*," he said, sweeping me into the air and spinning me around and around until we were both so dizzy we fell all over each other laughing.

But when I got to the dressing room and began peeling off my tights, I started feeling sad again. Joey would be dancing with Ballet on the Beach and Paterson was leaving early for college classes. I was thinking about how I was the only one with nothing to look forward to, when Paterson raced in. "You'll never believe who's here."

"Who? Baryshnikov?"

"No," she whispered. "It's Gray."

How was that possible? I'd resigned myself to the fact that I wouldn't see him for months, maybe not even then. I stuffed my tights into my bag and raced out of the dressing room. Gray was standing by the exit of the auditorium. I threw my arms around him and shrieked, "What are you doing here?"

He laughed. "You were great."

"Thanks," I said, smiling. I let go of him, suddenly

struck silent. He took that moment to pull a small gold box out of his pocket and hand it to me.

My fingers trembled as I removed the lid and then the tiny cotton square. I saw the gold chain first and lifted it out of the box. Dangling from the bottom of the chain was a pair of tiny red slippers.

"I found it at a museum gift shop," Gray said. "I thought you might like it." He unhooked the chain and leaned toward me as he fastened the clasp. My insides fluttered like tiny *bourrées*. Just as I looked up at him, I caught sight of Melissa, leaving the auditorium. She took one look at us and stormed off, looking more like an ugly stepsister than a ballerina.

I didn't get a chance for a long while to tell Gray how much I loved the necklace. My lips were otherwise occupied.

Paterson leaned across the table. "How long is he here for?"

I smiled. "The whole summer. His private school in New York is out and his mom has more work to do down here. They can keep the house for three more months."

Paterson gave a thumbs-up as Gray and Joey returned to the booth.

Gray slid beside me while Joey scooted next to Paterson.

"So what's going on with Ballet on the Beach?" Gray said. "What's your first ballet?"

Joey hesitated. "*Sleeping Beauty.*"

Paterson groaned. "Haven't you learned *anything* these past two months?"

Joey threw up his hands. "Hey, Kayla's the one that's destined to change the world of dance." He looked at me. "Are you sure you don't want to have that surgery and join me next year? I'm really going to miss dancing with you."

"Right now, I'm sure. Someday I might pay Dr. Marlowe another visit. But it'll be because *I* want it done, not because someone else tells me I have to."

Paterson clapped. "Spoken like a true feminist. I've finally converted you."

"Maybe," I said. "I have to think about it a little more."

Gray put his arm around me. "I brought you some more brochures about colleges and dance companies in New York. I'll show them to you later."

Joey put down his menu and announced, "If you're going to keep them, then you have to give them names."

We all stared at him. "Give what names?" I said.

"You know, your boobs. Like Thelma and Louise or something like that."

I shook my head. "Too violent. It reminds me of those women in that Austin Powers movie who started shooting bullets from their nipples."

Everyone laughed. "I've got one," Paterson said. "How about Monet and Manet?"

Gray, who had been staying out of the discussion, chimed in. "She can't give them men's names, even though they—the men, that is—were famous artists."

I thought for a minute. "I've got it. Lucy and Ethel."

Everyone was quiet for a second. Then Joey gave me a high five and everyone joined in, laughing.

I looked down at the shiny red shoes hanging between my breasts and leaned back into the curve of Gray's elbow. Lucy and Ethel. If there's one thing I've learned from them, it's that you've got to have a sense of humor.